Night Hawk's Witch

Alien Encounters, Book 3

Jo Hammers

Paranormal Crossroads & Publishing

Night Hawk's Witch

TABLE OF CONTENTS

Night Hawk's Witch

Alien Encounters, Book 3

Jo Hammers

CHAPTER ONE

Rio Rosa's Demise

Moon Dance and Tall Willow, having walked away from their previous human lives on adjoining ranches in Arizona, followed the bank of the Rio looking for new bodies to enter. They needed new identities plus human vehicles to dwell in while they waited for their opportunity to return to their individual home planets, Weelo and Plutonia. Time was of the essence. They could not survive for more than twenty-four hours in the Earth's atmosphere without a body covering to protect themselves.

Tall Willow, a Plutonian, had arrived on Earth by light port. Moon Dance, a Weelo, was stranded on Earth due to her mother ship, Noah I, crashing and being washed away in a horrendous flooding of Earth waters. Tall Willow was a scientist who was on a research and harvesting mission, secretly taking humans for specimens. Moon Dance was waiting for another mother ship to come for her. She had survived on Planet Earth by stepping down thru the centuries healing and living in discarded human corpses. She was also a scientist and had powers of healing and making human bodies live again. When Noah I crashed, she had been part of a harvesting crew. Her planet's vegetation and wild life was vanishing, and her Weelo people had almost quit reproducing. She had been trying to introduce new plants and wild animals onto her planet as well as do experiments in the field of reproduction, using human specimens as surrogate mothers. Her planet's women were losing more babies than they were managing to carry to the point of delivery. Moon Dance's life as a scientist ceased when Noah I crashed. Survival on Planet Earth amongst humans became her one focus.

Planets Weelo and Plutonia are neighboring planets, close enough for there to be trade and travel between the two. Moon Dance and Tall Willow had the same body types as humans, except they could be seen thru and could fly. They were filmy beings, having blue and purple skin. Both could not survive the Earth's atmosphere un less they entered a discarded human body like it was a space suit. A law of space and the universe stated that Weelo and Plutonian beings could not take and occupy a human body space suit that already had a spirit being living in it. Only dead, abandoned, human bodies could be taken at will. In other words, they could not enter a body that already had a being in it. Weelo and Plutonians outside of their space crafts had to look for, enter, and use human body space suits to survive the Earth's atmosphere. The acceptable space suits were freshly discarded corpses or new conceptions where the soul of a human spirit being had not entered yet.

Moon Dance in her previous incarnation, lived in a discarded human body and existence known as Sleeping Moon, a female member of a crazy rancher family who lived to pull pranks on each other. Sleeping Moon, a human, had been a young woman with a heart condition that was spoiled and waited on hand and foot by her family. Moon Dance entered her body when she died in the hospital. Repairing the bad heart, she assumed the life and identity of the girl. However, Moon Dance and her new host family did not gel. Feeling she had to find a different host body to keep from going crazy from putting up with Sleeping Moon's family, she walked away into the dessert and abandoned that human space suit body in the desert. Tall Willow, also an alien, did the same after being rejected by the older female of the same family. So, the two aliens, although different in some ways, formed an alliance and decided to enter their next human existences together for companionship. Tall Willow was a purple skin. Moon Dance had the blue skin of her planet's people. Taking bodies and living human existences, they both appeared to be pink skinned humans.

Moon Dance, having just abandoned her old life as a ranch girl named Sleeping Moon, flew down to the banks of the Rio Grande to take a peek at a Hispanic Tarot reader named Rio Rosa that was rumored to have a third eye in the middle of her forehead. Weelo and Plutonians had a third eye in the middle of their foreheads when they weren't hiding inside human forms. Moon Dance hoped that Rio Rosa was possibly another Weelo alien like herself. She was lonely for home and companionship. Humans in the area believed that Rio Rosa was a witch and her third eye was what she looked into the Tarot with.

Floating in the air down by the Rio, Moon Dance spotted an antiquated, silver sided, bullet shaped, travel trailer parked beside a sad looking Weeping Willow tree. She had heard White Eagle, one of two brothers she was cursed with in her former rancher family, had laughed and made jokes about Rio Rosa the bone rattler to aggravate his brother Night Hawk who was dating Rio Rosa and seriously thinking about marrying her. Moon Dance just had to set her mind at rest before leaving the area and embracing a new existence elsewhere.

Tall Willow, a Plutonian scientist and Moon Dance's current traveling companion, was on an Earth mission studying the internal reproductive organs of humans. His planet had a serious illness running rampant, called the Lavender Plague. His planet was considering using healthy, human specimens to mate with, possibly creating a future generation of Plutonians that were free of the plague, which was incurable. Human mate specimens would not rear the half breed children, they would just produce them. He had arrived by light port on Earth and the light ports only returned once each Earth year of time. Tall Willow had missed his light port ride home to his planet. Like Moon Dance, he was looking for a human body to enter and host him till next year's light port flight came.

As Moon Dance, in her blue, filmy, form floated above the bullet shaped trailer belonging to Rio Rosa, Tall Willow was trying to decide whether to take time out to join Moon Dance in taking a peep at the human witch named Rio Rosa who could possibly be an alien like them; if her third eye was real. Tall Willow, like Moon Dance, had less than 24 hours to find a discarded human body, enter it, repair it, and restart its life systems. He was a practical man and decided following a whim of curiosity was not the best course to pursue.

"Moon Dance, it is imperative that we move on down the Rio. We don't know how far we must travel before we find a new, deceased, human body to host us. We are nowhere near a hospital or a highway where there might be a wreck with fatalities. We have two bodies to find, not one." Tall Willow cautioned as he floated next to Moon Dance in his purple, filmy, form. Weelo had blue skin. Plutonians had purple skin.

"Rumors back at the ranch say that Rio Rosa down there has a third eye like us. Is it possible that she could be like us, a stranded alien from somewhere?"

"It is a possibility. However, she could just be a human with a scar on her forehead. I share your curiosity, but my need for a body host supersedes my curiosity. Also, there is the possibility that she may not be friendly. I have heard locals at times refer to her as a bitch." Tall Willow stated.

"You are probably right!" Moon Dance stated pausing for a moment in thought before continuing. "White Eagle, back on the ranch, told me that Rio Rosa below had a huge mole removed from her forehead leaving an eye shaped scar. He spoke of her gluing a jewel in the center of the scar and making it appear to be a third eye and hide her surgery flaw."

Suddenly, the door of the travel trailer flew open below and light streamed from its door. Then a figure exited the door in a hurry and sprinted toward the desert.

"Why is that woman running like a mad woman from Rio Rosa's trailer?" Tall Willow asked pointing at the human female who was running like hell into the dessert.

"She is probably a border crosser that Rio Rosa has possibly threatened with a gun." Moon Dance replied as she floated above the silver travel trailer. "The Tarot reader and bone rattler below does live on the bank of the Rio Grande.

"The running woman doesn't look Mexican!" Tall Willow retorted. "She has pale pink human skin and blonde, barfly hair."

"Something must be wrong." Moon Dance stated watching the running woman throw a knife into the desert. "I am going down and peep at Rio Rosa to see if she is okay."

"We really don't have the time, Moon Dance. We have less than twenty four hours to find new bodies."

"You go on, Tall Willow. I am going to float down and just take a quick peep to see if Rio Rosa is okay. If you find a host body before I catch up with you, enter it and start its life functions. Afterward, meet me back here in a few days. After peeping at Rosa, I will seek out a host body, enter, restart its life functions, and then return here to meet you."

Tall Willow put his spirit arms around Moon Dance. "I need you for a companion. Don't do anything foolish! Give yourself plenty of time to find a slinky, gorgeous human body to dwell in." He laughed loving the slinky part.

"Slithering, slinky, human, female bodies are not my style." She shot back rolling her eyes at him. Men were all alike. "I think I will choose a human body that has been fed well this time. Then I won't have to put up with Plutonian jerks like you hitting on me."

"Your point is taken. I would rather you, my new companion, not be starved to death and considering me as steak for your dinner."

"What do you mean by that?" She asked in a confused voice.

"I was just referring to the fact that the inhabitants of your home planet are cannibals." He replied. "Don't take offense at my ribbing."

"Planet Weelo is made up of vegetarians, I beg your pardon. I have had to eat animal flesh on Earth out of necessity. However, it is not my choice for food." Moon Dance replied in a huff.

"You have been gone from your Planet Weelo for several thousand years, Moon Dance. Societies of people change and evolve." He stated and then paused for a moment searching for words before continuing. "Your planet has evolved into a society of cannibals who harvest and eat human and each other's flesh."

"That is ridiculous, Tall Willow. My planet is an advanced and highly intelligent one. I doubt they have taken a step backwards in the evolution process to become flesh eating, wild animals." She huffed.

"You have been gone from your planet way too long, Moon Dance. There are slaughter houses on your planet Weelo that run around the clock, processing harvested human flesh for consumption."

"That can't be!" Moon Dance replied in disgust while instantly thinking of Gray Feather who had returned to Planet Weelo with her tribe. "Planet Weelo is an advanced society."

"Your planet has no vegetation or wild animals left on it. Weelo society has turned to harvesting and eating humans out of necessity."

"Are you serious?" She asked Tall Willow in disbelief.

"While you have been stranded here on Earth, your home planet has become a barren wasteland. Weelo's plants and animals are extinct from over harvesting. Your planet's population has dwindled due to lack of proper nutrition. They now eat a straight diet of meat and are at the point of possibly turning on each other. There is a serious shortage of food on your planet."

"Please tell me you are spoofing me." Moon Dance replied in disgust.

"The people on your planet, Moon Dance, exist on human flesh they have harvested from here on Earth and other similar, small, planets. Your home planet has no vegetation, animals, or insects. They have all been eaten. The cannibalistic situation has become so bad that travel between my planet and yours has almost ceased. Soon, Plutonian airways and light ports will be closed to Weelo like yourself.

"If what you are telling me is correct, I may be permanently stranded here on Earth if I don't take the next light port home with you and then catch one of the last flights going to Planet Weelo."

I would say that a year is possibly all you have, if you want to get home before all planets in your home's galaxy close their airways, light ports, and other means of transportation to the people of your planet. My planet Plutonia, which is the nearest sphere to you, fears an invasion from your cannibals wanting to harvest them for meat. The Great Mother Ship, Noah II, has made her last voyage to Earth. The other planets will not let her enter their airspaces to fuel. She sets idle and will not fly again. There will be no future rescue or harvesting ships making their way to Earth.

"You are telling me that I truly am stranded permanently on Earth, if I don't go home in the next light port with you!"

"Both of our planets are dying off. Yours has literally eaten its vegetation, animals, and population into almost extinction. My planet is plagued by the lavender disease causing us not to reproduce. Both of our home planets' populations are dwindling; yours due to cannibalism and mine due to lack of births. Your planet harvests humans for food and mine harvests them for reproduction specimens. We are mating with them. We would rather have half breed, slightly less intelligent Plutonian children, than no future generation at all. Your planet's populace assumes that your harvesters will keep supplying them with meat. Your planet's ships are old and new ones are not being built. It is just a matter of time till la-la land is over for the populace of your planet and they will discover that if they want to survive, they will have to kill and eat each other. Then a spiral downward will occur till there is but one man left standing and he will die from starvation. In my opinion, unproductive members of your society are already being sent secretly to the slaughter houses along with the humans."

"Are you telling me that the inhabitant's of my planet are eating each other, as well as harvested human flesh?"

"There are no elderly, sick, deformed, mentally slow, or menopausal age women now left on your planet, according to Plutonian guards who now are present on all light ports coming and going. That is where I have got my information concerning your planet. The guards are there because of the feared invasion from your planet possibly starting on Earth by entering our light ports."

"That is unfathomable!"

"According to the guards, the food chain on your planet is like falling dominoes. In a matter of months or a couple of years, the population of your planet will no longer be able to harvest humans or other planet beings for food. When the slaughter houses cease to run, your Weelo populace will start eating each other in the streets to survive. I personally think that thousands of Weelo have already disappeared into the food chain."

"Weelo had seven billion people on it when I left. How many live there now, in your opinion."

"My guess is about four million and most of them in the cities." Tall Willow replied. "I know the decline of your planet is a hard thing to swallow. However, you must consider that there is the possibility that the tribe from the New Mexico desert who went home without you have probably sent straight to the slaughter houses. All crime on planet Weelo now has one punishment, being sent to the slaughter houses. It is the ultimate death penalty. No one wants to think about being eaten. Also, you know that entering a space flyer before its captain, on your planet, is considered a felony. Your New Mexico tribe is guilty of that."

"I did not consider that on the day the Great Mother Ship came for us. My emotions were out of control and I just was not thinking straight." Moon Dance replied biting her lip. She may have caused the death of her entire tribe, including Gray Feather. She regretted her action, but had no heart to feel sorry for those who had disrespected her. She had given the shattered pieces of her heart to the hands of the dream catcher's web before leaving the ranch. She was no longer capable of deep feelings.

"I live by the laws of my Planet. Your tribe should have adhered to the laws of yours." Tall Willow replied. "Had they carried you in your dead human body into the airplane first, they would have been okay. Entering before you and leaving you in the desert to die is a crime."

"I would not have sent my tribe home, had I been thinking straight." Moon Dance spit out. "I now have no feelings for them, but I do regret being the cause of so many possible deaths in the slaughter houses."

"Your cannibal society is now at the point of speedy, spiraling downward. Unless you go home with me by light port next year, you might not ever make it home to your Planet Weelo; not that I advise going there. The guards on the light ports are predicting that your planet will be totally void of life and enter a dust bowl age in about three Earth years of time. It will not take long for four million people to devour each other."

"Why would you consider taking me back with you, to your planet, knowing that I am a Weelo?" She asked in shock. "Your planet is readying itself to fight against a possible Weelo invasion of my skin color. I will stick out like a sore thumb."

"Home is home! Everyone wants to go home to die. Should my planet be invaded by your planet's cannibals, I desire to be there to do my part in defending it. I am sure you feel the same about yours. We are what we are. Travel between our two planets still currently exists for dignitaries, the rich, newsmen, and scientists. You are a famous Weelo Scientist. No one will question your presence on my planet where scientists are still cooperating and trying to come up with solutions for your planets shortage of food and my planets reproduction problems. However, a year from now in my guess, all Weelo will be deported back to their planet just before the invasion starts. If you manage to make it home to Plutonia with me, you will have an automatic deportation flight home to Weelo."

"Even if I go home with you to your Plutonia, there is the possibility that I have no Weelo home or New Mexico tribe to go home to," Moon Dance muttered. "Is there?"

"A week or so stay on your home planet, Weelo, is all I would recommend. The population could turn on itself at any time and start eating each other to survive. The chance of you having any living relatives or old Weelo friends left on Weelo is not very good." He replied. "In my opinion, as a scientist, there is no hope for your planet since the downward spiral of eating its own kind has already started. As I said before, the children, the mentally challenged, the physically challenged, all older adults, criminals, and the welfare minded individuals of your planet are missing. There is only one explanation for the disappearance of millions of people. They have been killed in the slaughter houses and eaten by the unsuspecting citizens of Weelo."

"Your planet, Plutonia, is half the size of Weelo. Why is it surviving? You said it was at the point of extinction to."

"My planet is surviving its plague of the lavender disease by accepting humans into our race as mates. Marriage between pure, purple bloods is now against the law. The human race is breathing new life into our race. Some of the children born are free of the lavender disease. They are our future. When those children reach the mating age, they will be mated with the healthy of Plutonia and we will eradicate, hopefully, the lavender plague. Anyone with the lavender plague is being sterilized out of necessity.

"I am unfamiliar with this current plague of yours. What are its symptoms?" Moon Dance asked

"The main symptom is dotted skin, spots bigger than a rash. There is an itch to it and babies with it cry incessantly. My race is mating with humans. I wanted to take Song Bird home with me as my human mate. As you know, that didn't work out. When I told and showed her who I was, she accused me of being a Kachina, one of her mythical Native American demons."

"Before I was stranded on Earth due to the Noah I's crash, planet Weelo had garden green house ships capable of sustaining a thousand people each. Why would the elite of my planet, those with access, embrace cannibalism?"

"When Weelo started its spiral downward, evolving from a planet of vegetarians to one of meat eaters, a break down and a split in your Planet's government took place. The vegetarians, in possession of the garden ships, secretly flew the special crafts to far planet ports and did not return. The vegetarian elite of old planet Weelo entered the ships by night and were gone before the side that had started eating humans were aware of it. The meat eaters wanted to convert the garden ship to harvesters. Anyway, no garden ships now exist on your planet. Also, only two Mother Ships now exist on Weelo. Both are antiquated and in need of repairs. They are past the stage of making long flights and belong in a space ship salvage yard."

"So, there is the possibility that there are a few pure Weelo out there on garden ships somewhere." Moon Dance muttered looking up at the starry sky.

"Yes . . . . There were ten garden ships when they disappeared. That is a hundred thousand people total, if all survived. It is very possible the vegetarians have chosen some compatible, remote planet and started over as a new civilization of Weelo. They could have a population of a thousand or a hundred thousand; or they may have succumbed to strange diseases on other planets, that they have no immunity against, and have ceased to be."

"Song Bird's daughter disappeared in the desert after hearing a humming. Night Hawk and White Eagle are her children. Do you think she was harvested for meat or possibly a reproduction specimen by one of our two planets?"

"Hopefully, she is on my planet, Moon Dance, and mated to one of our disease free males. If so, she is safe from cannibals. However, there is a dark side to being mated with one of us. In order to increase our population with lavender disease free children, our disease free males are required to take as many wives as they can support. Being one of four to a dozen wives is the same as being some farmer's prize sow on Earth. Human women are like sows and required to produce as many children as possible. There is no birth control available for the human wives. They give birth just about every year. Even that, however, is preferable to being eaten on Planet Weelo."

"Your planet will survive extinction from making your choices, even though the thought of women being forced to reproduce appalls me. My planet will not survive do their choices. You don't know how that saddens me."

"I am a male citizen of Plutonia and a scientist. I know the importance of re-populating our planet. I will do my part to rid my planet of its plague and see that we, as a planet, have a future. That will include taking whatever human mates my government appoints me. There will be no choosing mates. I will mate with what-ever female humans, young, old, pretty, or homely that my planet appoints me to do so with. My off spring will be half-breeds, conceived out of necessity and not love. I am a patriot and will do my part to see that my Plutonian race survives."

"What about Song Bird? How could you have ever considered taking her home with you, knowing you would be taking four to twelve wives besides her?"

"Song Bird is my weak spot. I never expected to fall in love with a human. She isn't a scientist or highly intelligent. There was just something about her that I became addicted to. When I slept with her, she made me feel like I was the great-est man that ever existed. She became my drug of choice, as humans put it. I can't explain what it was like to be in her arms. No Plutonian woman had ever made me feel that way. Humans call the experience love. I call it an unbelievable utopian state drug."

"Wow. I have never had a man feel that way about me. I should be so lucky." Moon Dance replied.

"My falling in love with Song Bird just happened." He replied staring away into the distance as though he were thinking about her. "You are right. I can see that now. She would not have understood me having multiple wives besides her on Plutonia. Even though I am crazy about Song Bird, she is long past the age of be-ing a reproducing, human female. As a patriot and loyal citizen of Plutonia, I will sleep with however many appointed wives I am given nightly in order to produce my quota of disease free children."

"As a scientist, I understand what you are saying to me. As a friend of Song Bird, I am thankful she ran from you thinking you were a Kachina. She would never have understood you sleeping with someone other than her. Had she gone with you, she would have eventually died on your planet with a broken heart. Your drug of addiction would have ceased to be potent. She would have thrown you permanently from her bed and arms."

"As scientists, Moon Dance, we have to do what is best for our individual planets. I should have returned home years ago and done my part in fathering our future race. I could have adult, half-breed Plutonian, scientist sons by now. My love for Song Bird has kept me here on Earth. Until now, love has clouded my thinking. When the next light port appears, I will board and go home leaving her behind. You are welcome to accompany me."

"Love blinded me to, Tall Willow. My human Song Bird was named Gray Feather." Moon Dance replied thinking of Gray Feather and the obsessive love she once had for him. Now, he was just memories because she no longer had a heart to experience the emotions that accompanied being obsessed with and attracted to someone. Her relationship was like a dull movie. She could play it and watch it in her mind, but it stirred no emotions in her. "I accept your invitation to accompany you home in the light port. It is a generous offer on your part."

"As scientists, you and I understand each other and our allegiance to our planets and their problems. As a scientist, I want to see you return to Planet Weelo, even though it is too late for you to attempt to stop its downward spiral. That, Moon Dance, is why I am willing to take you home to Plutonia with me. It is my respect for you as a fellow scientist."

"I won't forget this, Tall Willow. If I were human, I would agree to be one of your appointed wives, reproduce, and help rid your planet of the lavender disease. I respect you that much. However, I am not human. I am a blue skinned Weelo."

Tall Willow pulled Moon Dance's face to him and kissed her on the cheek. "Would you consider being a secret wife, till the impending Weelo invasion has come and gone?" He asked with a smirk. "As scientists, we could be good together; although you would rarely find me in your bed. I do have to help father a new civilization."

"Get out of here!" Moon Dance retorted play slapping him on his cheek. "An affair with you, I might consider. However, I will never be any male's secret mistress.

Tall Willow laughed heartily. Then he flew away in a flash, following the Rio to look for a human host body. Weelo and Plutonians could fly. However, they had no wings. They were like the caped, human, super, comic book heroes that flew with the speed of light. They were advanced alien beings, not angels.

CHAPTER TWO

Bartering For A Body

After watching Tall Willow streak thru the sky till he was out of sight, Moon Dance floated down to the silver bullet shaped travel trailer belonging to Rio Rosa and circled it peeping in the windows. The lights were all on, but the travel trailer was eerily quiet. As she floated around to the rear, she was suddenly frightened as a pinkish spirit being shot thru an open window there. It was a human spirit who was equally as surprised to see her.

"Who are you? Are you with her?" The pink, human, female spirit asked in an angry, frightened shout while pointing to the desert where a female intruder had run.

"My name is Moon Dance. I was traveling the astral above your travel trailer when I spotted what appeared to be a female border crosser exiting your trailer and running in a frenzy into the desert. I floated down to see if there was anyone in the trailer needing help. Before exiting my human body, I used to carry a handgun in my pocket for border crossers."

"It wasn't a border crosser that surprised me, stabbed me to death, and then ran from my trailer. It was a cheap female tramp who works at the café in town." She stated annoyed. Then a tear rolled down her spirit face. "It just doesn't seem fair. I worked my butt off in that travel trailer reading tarot cards to make myself a living. A pregnant, jealous, bimbo tramp did me in, to keep me away from her man, as she called him. I just paid that travel trailer off. Isn't that a kick in the teeth?" The pink human spirit sputtered. After taking a moment to calm down, she asked. "Is this purgatory?"

"You are in the astral, the crossing over realm. Are you, by any chance, Night Hawk's witch?" Moon Dance asked knowing that the female spirit was not Weelo or Plutonian. She did not have a third eye. If she was a human witch, she was a fake one. She had no third eye to look into and read the hearts and thoughts of Earth men.

"That figures . . . ," the pink spirit muttered. "No easy or straight shot to Heaven for me. I have always had to look out for myself. No man on Earth ever gave a real damn about me and apparently I am on my own here as well. Who in the hell are you?"

"My name is Moon Dance." I replied. "You are . . . ?"

"Just call me Rio Rosa." The pink human spirit shot back and after a short pause added. "I was a rattler of chicken bones and a reader of the tarot before that blonde bimbo did me in."

"I am pleased to meet you, Rio Rosa. I just exited a human body also. I lived in the body of your Night Hawk's sister, Sleeping Moon, for a short time. I laid her body down in the desert."

"Are you telling me that you are the spirit of Sleeping Moon, Night Hawk and White Eagle's sick, twisted, egotistical, spoiled, rich, brat of a sister?"

"Sleeping Moon died in the operating room when she had her heart surgery. I guess you might say I am a Kachina, for search of a better word. I entered Sleeping Moon's dead body in the hospital, revived it, and have lived the last three or so months in it. Her spirit has flown off to who knows where. I discarded her body in the desert earlier and I am now looking for another. I was not happy on the ranch. Her brothers were lived and breathed to see what craziness they could pull on each other. I found them to be very annoying and I just got tired of putting up with them."

"I can understand you not wanting to be a part of that crazy family. I was night Hawk's lover till a couple of nights ago. I once thought he was in love with me and that I was more than just a roll in a travel trailer bunk to him. Boy . . . was I a fool. He had several secret ladies in his bunk when I was not around. The woman that ran from here, after killing me, is a cheap, bar fly waitress named Millie. She came here demanding that I stay away from Night Hawk. I tried to tell her that I had broken up with him. We argued. She was drunk and pulled a knife on me. Now, here I am." Rio stated throwing her arms in the air in disgust. Shaking her head, she pointed down to her travel trailer. "I planned to hook on to that trailer tomorrow, move on down the Rio, and start over somewhere. Thanks to Millie the bimbo, I am starting over. However, it is without my paid for silver streamlined travel trailer."

"Why don't you just reenter your body, repair it, and go on with your life?" Moon Dance asked.

"Human spirits can't do that. Once out of our bodies, we must return to Hell or Heaven. "The Catholic nuns, at the orphanage I was raised in, kept telling me there was a purgatory. Apparently, they were right. I have found it. The orphanage was my hell and that paid for travel trailer down there was my Heaven. Now, Millie has sent me here to purgatory. I never expected the devil to be a blonde, bimbo, eight months pregnant woman."

"If you do not intend to re-enter your human body, how would you feel if I should take up habitation in it? I have the capabilities of repairing your discarded human body, once I am in it. I cannot gain light port passage home for almost a year. I need a human host body to survive in till I return home by light port in a year."

"Why would you choose my discarded human form? I was one ugly woman with a huge, tea cup sized growth on my forehead. Kids made fun of me and adults stared and whispered. My childhood and early adulthood were miserable. No one would hire me, I was so ugly. I stole a deck of Tarot Cards from a bookstore and taught myself to read them. I have read a lot of cards and rattled a lot of chicken bones to make enough money to have my growth removed. After the operation, I was left with a huge eye shaped scar on my forehead. I learned to live with it by making it appear to be a third eye, a witch's eye. Night Hawk always told me it didn't matter to him. I was so starved for anyone to care about me. Like a fool, I fell for his lines. I had plans tomorrow. I was moving on down the Rio. Thanks to Night Hawk's very pregnant lover, I will never have the chance to know true love."

"I heard about your third eye and thought perhaps you were a Weelo spirit like me. I am sorry that I did not make my way down here to the Rio to meet you before your unfortunate death. I needed a friend and apparently you did also. I am really sorry. Like you, I have been walked on by the man I loved."

"Did Night Hawk tell you about me?"

"No . . . it was Charlie Elkhorn."

"Elkhorn has been down here a few times to see me. He inquires about his love life, or lack of one. I told him one day he would meet a Kachina and fall in love with her. He always told me I was crazy. However, he would always stay and have a beer or two with me. I was not Psychic, just a good reader of people. I have done some good guessing over the years. I had to fake it in order to have a means of making money to feed myself. There isn't much in the way of employment here along the Rio for a woman with a growth on her forehead the size of a teacup. Also, no man ever considered me as a woman. I was on my own. It was either rattle chicken bones or starve after I ran away from the orphanage at sixteen."

"How did you meet Night Hawk?" Moon Dance asked out of curiosity.

"Night Hawk brought his mother, Song Bird, here for a reading just after his mother, her daughter, disappeared. Law enforcement couldn't find her and the old woman was grasping at straws to find a way to locate her. He kept coming back on pretense of obtaining more information about his mother I know now he was just interested in sleeping with me, one more woman to pursue and add as a notch to his belt. He was fascinated with the jewel I wore in the scar on my forehead. I also think he liked spooking his friends out by eventually having a witch on his arm on Saturday nights. I see it now. His friends were all Native Americans and reared to fear Kachina. I was the crazy prank he was pulling on his friends. I just never realized it, till he dumped me for Millie the Barfly. He had been secretly seeing her the whole time he dated me. I was a fool."

"I am sorry he used you. I was once in love with a man named Gray Feather and he made me believe that he loved me. When my heart was racing for him, he slept with a going nowhere half breed and married my hair dresser. I didn't see it coming. "

"What about Charlie Elkhorn? Did he think you were my predicted Kachina that he would fall in love with?"

"He said he had fallen in love with me. However, when I unzipped Sleeping Moon's body and showed him me, a blue skinned Weelo Kachina that was living in and using Sleeping Moon's body as a host, he wet his jeans and ran." Moon Dance replied. "His Catholic side kicked in and he called me a demon!"

Rio Rosa laughed. "I wish I had been there. I might have made a few bucks making him medicine bags to ward off evil spirits and demon possession."

"In my current thinking, human men aren't worth wasting your time on."

"You have got that right!." Rio Rosa spit out in a disgusted voice. "When the chips are down, they run like hell or dump you for the nearest pretty face. In my case it was the blonde bimbo named Millie."

"Gray Feather first chose a half breed in our tribe named Pansy. I walked upon them making love and howling at the moon on the sand dune behind my tribe's camp in the desert. Then he married the oldest woman in our tribe, a hair dresser. I, apparently, was just a notch on his belt like you were on Night Hawk's. He whispered he loved me, but I wasn't number one or two in his life. I was nothing to him. It has been hard for me to admit that."

"We are two of a kind." Rio Rosa replied sighing. Then she added, "I will let you have my human body under certain conditions."

"What are they?" Moon Dance asked.

"You may repair and use my human body till you gain light port passage home. I will remain here in the purgatory in-between worlds and float about till that time. When you discard my repaired body, a year from now, I will re-enter it. You must agree to zip me up in my repaired human body and heal the body zipper so that I can live out my future life as Rio Rosa."

"That sounds reasonable." Moon Dance replied.

"There is a second condition. I wish to get even with Night Hawk for using me. I was in love with him and wanted children by him. He stabbed me in the back sleeping with others I was unaware of. I did not know about Millie or the others till tonight. Millie is pregnant by him. That was the ultimate slap to my face by him." Rio Rosa stated with tears in her spirit eyes.

"What do you wish me to do to him?" Moon Dance asked reluctantly. She was not a person who normally carried out vengeful acts towards others.

"You may have my body if you agree to flirt with and enter a relationship with his brother, White Eagle. I would like Night Hawk to discover me in the arms of someone else, and that person to be someone that would be equally a hurtful slap to his face. The two brothers having a life time of hard feelings for each other should be sufficient revenge. Night Hawk will be stuck with a pregnant, low class, bimbo waitress and memories of me slapping him with White Eagle. I want my human body to be pregnant with White Eagle's child when I reenter it."

"You don't know what you are asking! White Eagle is a kind and gentle man." Moon Dance replied.

"Take it or leave it." Rosa replied. "That body down there is my property."

"I will pass!" Moon Dance stated in disgust. "You are indeed a witch, Rosa. "

"It takes one to know one." Rio Rosa retorted. "If I were guessing, you would secretly like to have revenge on your Gray Feather guy who discarded you for his bimbos."

"Rosa, you cannot make Night Hawk love you. I could not make Gray Feather, my Night Hawk, choose me." Moon Dance replied. "We are two rejects who have to learn to deal with it, somehow. Revenge hurts more than just the person you are aiming at."

"You are right about the rejects part. However, I am willing to deal with the fall out. Leaving here and traveling pregnant on down the Rio is worth it to me. I have never had anyone. A child to love would be a luxury to me."

"As much as I need your discarded body, Rio Rosa, I cannot carry out your revenge. I am sorry!" Moon Dance stated and then shot off thru the night sky to look for another body.

After Moon Dance was gone, Rio Rosa had to make a choice. She could stay Earth bound and stand guard over a body she had always hated, or she could move on. After thinking about it, she decided her Earth existence was a total loss. Her only hope for revenge had been Moon Dance and she was gone. With a heavy sigh and a broken heart, she shot off into the universe to embrace whatever lay ahead. All was lost to her, even her discarded body.

CHAPTER THREE

Jack Meets Pansy Skywalker

Jack Benson had been desperately looking for a way to make his way back to Moon Dance. Traveling from Earth to planet Weelo in spirit form, he had accidentally found himself locked inside a dream portal and could not exit it. He could see Moon Dance from the portal by peeping thru Native American dream catchers wherever he found them. However, every time he tried to fly thru a dream catcher to return to her, the hands of the many webs would throw him back into the portal of dreams, nightmares, and time travel.

Jack Benson had been peeping thru Rio Rosa's dream catcher as Moon Dance bargained with Rio Rosa for her discarded body. In his thinking, it was now or never. He had to make his way back to her. He had once been in love with her before their Weelo ship, Noah I, had crashed thousands of Earth years earlier. He had something of hers that was a necessity. Taking a deep breath and clutching his chest where a piece of Moon Dance's heart was attached to his, he made another attempt to float thru and enter the Earth realm. Once more, it was fruitless. The hands of Rio Rosa's dream catcher web threw him violently back into the portal.

As he floated in the portal of nightmares, dreams, and time travel; he came to the conclusion that dream catcher ports were not the answer for making his way back to her. He was going to have to find another way to exit the light port he was in.

"What are you peeping at?" A female voice asked as she floated near him.

Surprised that someone was in the light portal besides him, he turned to see who was speaking to him. A spirit being was speaking to him that was a half breed. One side of her was blue filmy skinned like the Weelo and the other half of her was pink like that of humans.

"I am trying to find a way to exit this portal and return to Earth life. I entered this portal thru a dream catcher. Now, in spite of all my efforts to exit and return to Earth life, hands of the web keep throwing me back on this side of the veil." He spit out in annoyance.

"I am caught between worlds also. I was eaten by animals on Planet Weelo." The pink, female, half breed stated.

"That could not have been a pleasant death." Jack Benson replied. "Were you on Safari and attacked by a Weelo Planet bear or big cat?"

"Bears and big cats no longer exist on Planet Weelo. They have all been hunted and eaten. The animal eating me was a pure blood Weelo."

"You were eaten by a cannibal?" Jack asked and then quickly added before she had a chance to reply. "I hope the Weelo justice system threw the book at him."

"Courts and justice are now a laugh on Planet Weelo. There is only one sentence on Weelo. If you do something the populace finds despicable, you are sent to the food chain."

"I don't understand what you are trying to tell me." He replied. "What do you mean by the food chain?"

"I had just disembarked on Planet Weelo when I was hauled into Weelo court and then sent to the food chain because of my disrespect of a woman scientist named Moon Dance. I never would have taken the great ship Noah II home had I known what chaos and atrocities existed on Planet Weelo?"

"Are you talking about Moon Dance, the Weelo scientist who died just as the great ship arrived to rescue a group of New Mexico pure bloods or are you speaking of another scientist with the same name?"

"I spent many years in the New Mexico Desert surviving with the tribe of Weelo pure bloods that were passing themselves off as Native Americans. Moon Dance was our medicine woman. Being a half breed, I didn't have the third eye that let me understand who half of me really was or where I was from. Moon Dance to me at that time was just an aging old hag who tried to control everyone and always got what she wanted. I found a man wandering in an amnesia fog. I fell in love with him and took him home to the desert. Moon Dance would not let me keep him. She took him from me with no regards for my feelings for him. There was a law in our tribe that said if you found anything in the desert it was yours, no matter who it had formerly belonged to. She defied that law and took him for herself."

"Who was the fog man?" Jack asked knowing it had to be his former friend, Michael Haven who had disappeared and lived for several years in an amnesia state with a small tribe of Native American Indians in the New Mexico desert.

"I named him Gray Feather. When I found him he did not know who he was before that moment."

"So, in your thinking, he was your man because he was found by you?"

"He was mine by tribal law, but she took him from me and kept him for three or so years. The tribe stated I was a half breed and the law didn't apply to me. I was not happy about it."

"Knowing that you were a half breed, why did you take Noah II home?"

"Gray Feather was going. I could not see myself remaining behind on Earth without him. I was in love with him and he did nothing to save me from the slaughter house."

"If you were eaten, how did you end up here in this dream port?" Jack asked returning to the subject of cannibalism.

"We were all bound and hung on hooks in a Weelo processing plant, slaughter house. We were all zapped with a stun gun, put to sleep. In a brief moment of sleep before being slaughtered for meat, I entered the dream world or this light port. Some of the others on the slaughterhouse conveyor hooks did the same. We now exist here in this cage of a dream portal, but we have no bodies. We are all like bits of colored glass in a kaleidoscope. This dream portal or kaleidoscope has us caged. If we could escape it, we could find host bodies on Earth or other planets to live in again."

"What do you mean slaughter house?" He asked, not wanting to embrace the horrible truth she was speaking of. "Are you speaking of a meat processing plant like on Earth where they kill, butcher, and package beef, chicken, and pork for human consumption?"

"Plant life and animals no longer exist on Planet Weelo. They are extinct due to over harvesting. Two thirds of the inhabitants of Planet Weelo have died off due to malnutrition due to the lack of vitamins in their diet from plants. For awhile, the harvesting ships brought plants from other planets to supplement the diets of the leaders, scientists, and those deemed necessary for society's up keep. However, the mother ships are now old and in disrepair. The last ship to fly was the one who rescued us in the New Mexico desert. The working class, those who once serviced the ship, was not given plant life to eat and have died off. The leaders, scientists, and rich did not consider that they needed to feed and keep the lower class healthy. Now, there are no ships flying. Cannibalism has now taken over the planet. Those deemed unintelligent, criminals, sick, physically challenged, etc. are sent to the slaughter house. It is just a matter of time till the rich, intelligent, scientists, and leaders start turning on each other. Only about four hundred thousand pure Weelo exist now. The spiral downward from cannibalism has now started.

The last man standing will starve to death."

"Are you serious?" Jack asked in disgust. The thought of eating human or Wee-lo flesh repulsed him.

"See that group of blue skinned spirits over there?" She asked pointing to a group of five filmy blue spirits floating about in the portal.

"Yes, I see them."

"They were slaughtered also."

"My name is Jack Benson. Who are you?" He asked.

"My name is Pansy Skywalker."

"Who are the five floating Weelo spirits behind you?"

"Hissing Cat, Running Deer, Cactus flower, Humming Bird, and Honey Bee. We all were sentenced to the food chain on returning home to Weelo. We were slaughtered like hogs for our disrespect of a Captain Moon Dance. Finding a way to exit this dream portal and then finding host bodies is our only hope of existing again." Pansy answered as she eyed Jack wondering who he was. "Who are you?"

"I am Dr. Benson, a colleague and friend of Gray Feather. I think we might have met back in the desert in New Mexico. I chose to stay behind with Moon Dance and care for her dead body."

"What do you mean stay behind? You entered the space flyer after we all had boarded, carrying the old witch's corpse. You carried her to the captain's seat and then closed the curtain so none of us could see what you were doing with her. The space flyer took off. When we landed in the bay of the Great Mother ship, Noah II, you and Moon Dance were not on board."

"Moon Dance was not dead. Her human body was dead, but she was alive inside of that body. She was waiting till all of you were gone to exit the human body and be free of all of you."

"That figures. She probably knew we would all receive a death sentence for being on her craft without her." Pansy Skywalker huffed. "How did you end up here in this dream portal? You weren't with us in the slaughter house line."

"I entered here from the Earth Realm, and like you, I can't seem to find a way to go back." Jack replied not wanting to offer any information as to Native American dream catchers being doors, portals, and gates.

"Be thankful you didn't go home to Planet Weelo without Captain Moon Dance."

Pansy stated sarcastically. "I have personally learned what happens to those who disrespect her. However, I also know what the word revenge means. Should I ever make it back to earth and find myself a host body to exist in again, I am going to be her worst nightmare if I can find her."

"Do you know anything as to whether my two friends on the space flyer are alive or dead?"

"Who are you speaking of?"

"Michael Haven Gray Feather and Doctor Ralph Archer . . . ," Jack Benson replied.

"Gray Feather, Ralph Long Legs, some human children, and my child named Carol Sue live in animal cages in the Weelo Zoo. They will remain there till the public loses interest in them. Weelo children no longer exist. Due to a meat only diet, the women have quit reproducing. The four human children are caged like monkeys and viewed liked those in Earth zoos. Your friends are viewed as though they were apes. There are no males, to speak of, on Weelo now. Weelo is a planet of women. Your friends are male specimens in the zoo. Many Weelo women, especially the younger ones, have never seen a man. That is the reason your friends are alive. When the public loses interest in them, they will be sent to the slaughter house and eaten just like we were."

Jack Benson turned and looked at the group of blue filmy skinned alien beings with three eyes who were floating behind Pansy Skywalker. "Which one of you is Hissing Cat?" He asked eyeing them.

"I am Hissing Cat!" A gorgeous, blue, alien being stated as she approached him. She was far more attractive than those with her, although she looked to be older.

"Are you the Hissing Cat that lived in human form on Earth and married Michael Haven Gray Feather in the desert of New Mexico before returning on Noah II to Planet Weelo?"

"I am she. Who are you?"

"I am Jack Benson, Gray Feather's Earth doctor friend. I also am Weelo like you. I once, thousands of years ago, was a doctor on Noah I before it crashed."

"You don't look like a doctor to me." Pansy Skywalker smirked. "What were you a lowly, little, hair ball remover, cat doctor like Gray Feather? He seems to have a thing for low class hissing cats."

"Watch it, Pansy. This Cat will claw your eyes out if you mess with me." Hissing Cat replied. "He married me. You can't say the same."

Pansy Sky walker shot off into the in-between world in a huff having been put down by Hissing Cat.

"So, you were a doctor on Noah I. I don't recall ever bumping into you." Hissing Cat threw out.

"That is because I was prematurely bald and didn't have the need of a hair dresser." Jack retorted.

"Well, I never had need of a doctor. I guess we are even on that one!" Hissing Cat replied sarcastically. Besides, I would have never chosen to see a bald headed doctor. A smart woman doesn't trust her health issues to a doctor who can't even cure his own baldness?"

"Your point is taken." Jack replied rolling his eyes in disgust at the hair dresser who was full of herself as well as getting the best of him in their war of words. She pleased him, but he would never tell her so. He liked a woman who wasn't afraid to speak her mind. If he hadn't made a commitment to return to Moon Dance, he just might have an affair with the hair dresser, after he managed to catch her. He was sure that Hissing Cat would be easier to catch than Moon Dance."

"Furthermore, an intelligent Weelo man would know how to get thru these ports and avoid the hands guarding them. I assume you are probably a half-breed. They are a little slower in their thinking and can't figure a lot of things out. They go bald because they are too lazy to use their heads to get them out of bad situations such as this. They would be happy in this port just floating about and shining their bald heads. Do you wax and shine your bald head, Jack Benson?"

"Do you stand around sharpening your claws, Hissing Cat? You seem to have them out at the moment."

"You just wait Jack Benson." She huffed. "I will find a way to get out of this dream catcher portal and when I do I guarantee you that I will not take you with me."

"My feelings are the same Hissing Cat. Besides, what is so important on Earth that you are trying to make it back there? You are Weelo. Why not return there and enter some host body. I hear there are a few humans there for various reasons."

"Are you crazy, Jack Benson? The Weelo have turned cannibals and are eating each other. Humans were harvested for meat first. Now the population is about to turn on itself and eat each other due to food shortages. If I returned and entered a human body, if I could find one, I would be low man on the totem and sent to the slaughter house again. That was an experience I do not wish to replay, thank you! On Earth in a human body, I will at least be able to live without the fear of being eaten. It was a mistake going home to Planet Weelo."

"I am sorry you did not return to find Planet Weelo as it was in its Utopian days." Jack Benson replied eyeing her up and down. He liked what he saw."

"Put your eyes back in your head, Jack Benson. I don't go for bald headed idiots, who can't take a key and open their own door. I gather that the dream catcher port you are looking at is yours." She stated rolling her eyes at him. "Where is your key?"

"You are definitely not getting a key to my place." He replied giving her the eye. The truth was, he didn't have a key or a clue how to enter his own dream catcher passageway. However, he would not admit that to her. It was a good thing he was in love with Moon Dance. He would just have to show her what a man he was and he didn't need a key for that. Then, he looked away. He was seeing himself in bed with her. He felt like a cheating husband. He had made a commitment to returning to Moon Dance.

"Well, don't expect a key to my portal door when I find it." Hissing Cat replied looking him up and down. He was eye candy, except for his bald head. She could see herself explaining to her friends that he had lost all of his hair on the headboard of her bed. That wasn't all she saw happening between them. She blushed.

"Are my friends Michael and Ralph safe in the zoo from the cannibals?" He asked counting the shades of eye shadow she had layered on her eyes.

"They are on the food chain list. The public, I am sure, has about lost interest in them and have turned their attention to survival and finding food, not visiting zoos for pleasure. A growling stomach knows no pleasure. The children in the zoo will be eaten first. The planet now sees children as just extra mouths to feed."

"How long do you think the children have till they are sent to the slaughtering house?" Jack asked with his guts cringing. He had always wanted children, Weelo children.

"They may have already been sent to the slaughter house and eaten by the Weelo. There are no clocks or calendars here in the port and I am not sure how long I have been here. There is no sun to come up or sun to go down in here."

"Isn't there a mass exodus from Planet Weelo since it has succumbed to being a cannibalistic state?

"There is nowhere to go, Jack Benson. The nearest planets have closed their doors to immigrants. They fear an invasion of cannibals and then being eaten. The truth is, there are not enough men left on Planet Weelo to attack an airplane, much less a planet. The women have killed and eaten the men. Only studs for the male brothels are safe. The average Joe has gone into the food chain."

"There aren't any men on Weelo?" He asked in shock.

"On Earth, farmers keep one bull to service his cows. He has no need for more and sales off the younger ones to slaughter houses to be butchered for meat. That is the way it is on Planet Weelo. Twelve or so studs, bulls if you want to call them that, are kept to service the cows, the elite of society. Sex is for those who can afford it. The average young woman on Planet Weelo may never see a man in her lifetime. There are a couple of male brothels and they service only those of the higher classes of women. There are no men other than them on the planet. The studs are not Weelo. They are prisoners from other planets who have nowhere to go should they escape, and have no reason to try to take over as leaders of the planet. They are too small in numbers. All Weelo men have been killed and eaten. Weelo women are now like the Praying Mantis. They think nothing of eating their stud after he services them. Only the clever studs survive."

"Why were you sent to the food chain first?" Jack Benson asked. The Michael he knew would have not let his wife go before him. He would have taken her place and spared her as long as he could.

Hissing Cat didn't answer.

"Leave her alone, Jack Benson." Pansy Sky Walker stated harshly having returned to rejoin in on the conversation. "She has been subjected to the worst kind of betrayal. Your friend, Michael Gray Feather, did nothing to stop her from going to the slaughter house. She was his wife and he chose a stranger's children to save instead. He also betrayed me. Our night of passion on a sand dune meant nothing to him. "

"How did he betray you, Pansy Skywalker?" Jack Benson asked trying to put all their puzzle pieces together and figure out the fate of his two doctor friends.

"The zoo was to send me or my daughter Carol Sue to the slaughter house. Gray Feather. He begged for Carol Sue's life to be spared, like I was nothing to him. Carol Sue is nothing to him."

Jack was appalled at Pansy's reply. He could see in her eyes that she was a cold, self-centered, person that was not capable of having nurturing feelings toward a child. She had to be a sociopath who probably loved only one person, Gray Feather. Now, she felt betrayed by him. That was not a good thing for his friend Michael, should they ever cross each other's paths again.

Hissing Cat had visibly bit her lip to keep from saying anything. As Jack and Hissing cat refrained from speaking for a moment, a different spirit being floated over and joined in on the group's conversation. Jack Benson didn't recognize him.

"Is there a secret to getting past the hands of the web?" Asked the blue, male, being who stared into the web. "I have tried and tried to get thru, but the hands keep throwing me back on this side of the web. I have not figured out the key to get past the hands. What do you think the hands want?"

Jack was hesitant to answer his question in fear for Moon Dance's safety. He could see darkness and hatred in Pansy Skywalker's eyes. If allowed to return to Earth, she could become anyone's nightmare, including Moon Dance.

"I don't have a clue." Jack Benson replied in a lie. The stranger's words referring to a key had resonated with him. The web portal door didn't take a literal key. The hands wanted payment for traveling thru their webbed door. He grinned on the inside realizing he had figured out how to return to Moon Dance. Now, he just had to figure out what he had, as a spirit being, that he could give them. Also, he would have to wait till all of them got bored with him and went their way before he could attempt to cross back into the Earth Realm. He didn't want them to figure out the key. He feared for Moon Dance's safety, should they find her.

CHAPTER FOUR

Out of Luck

Moon Dance was frantic. It had been hours since her encounter with Rio Rosa. To her dismay, she had not been able to find a host body to enter. Her time limit, of twenty-four hours for searching, was running out. At the most, she had a couple of hours before she ceased to exist. On planet Weelo, her spirit was Eternal. On Earth, it was not. In desperation, she decided to return to the travel trailer on the Rio and accept Rosa's terms. She needed Rio Rosa's discarded body to survive.

About fifteen minutes before she was to cease to be, she arrived back at the travel trailer to find that paramedics had Rosa's bloody dead body on a stretcher with its head covered. They were about to take her away. Floating up to the stretcher at the back of the ambulance, she assessed the situation. When the paramedics had their head turned, she dove into the body of Rio Rosa like it was a swimming pool. After straightening out in the dead body and getting her bearings, she started its heart to beat and then repaired the stab wounds and internal injuries. Just as the paramedics were about to lift and slide the gurney she was on in to the back of the ambulance, Moon Dance started to kick and move the limbs of Rosa's body to let them know they did not have a corpse on their four wheeled stretcher.

"Uncover my head, you body snatchers. I, Rio Rosa, head witch of the Kachina have returned from the dead." Moon Dance shouted in an eerie, ghost like, voice projection. She knew that almost everyone in the area knew that Rio Rosa was a witch. She needed to carry on that image. "Uncover my head before I rattle your children's bones and snatch your soul."

"What the hell . . ." one of the paramedics stated uncovering Rio Rosa Moon Dance's face. "Oh my God, she is alive and giving me the Kachina evil eye." The older Native American paramedic stated and immediately jumped back knowing that the corpse of Rio Rosa had been dead for possible six to ten hours. Law enforcement and the coroner had already left after filling out her death certificate. Rio Rosa had been the victim of a homicide.

"This isn't good . . . she did not have a third eye in her forehead when I covered her with the sheet, just a great big surgery scar." The other paramedic added with his forehead breaking out in perspiration. In a nervous frenzy, he placed his fingers together and popped his knuckles.

"Where are my Tarot cards and chicken bones?" Moon Dance asked in a slow, low, voice to frighten the two, skittish, Native American paramedics.

"Does it matter if we ate the chicken off the bones before arriving here?" The younger of the two asked with big eyes. They had stopped on the way to the crime scene and bought some Southern fried chicken. They had eaten it on the way.

"This Kachina knows all and sees all. The two of you are doomed and may meet the Great White Spirit before dawn. Other black bird like Kachina, besides me, intends to eat your flesh and then rattle your bones. Death is now tracking the two of you like a black crow eyes a mouse scampering on the desert floor. You are soon to be meat for the gods. Do the two of you want to know where you are going to die?"

Neither of the paramedics answered her. They were big eyed and about to wet their jeans. Their dead corpse now had a real eye in the middle of its forehead and the eye had just winked at them. Only a scar graced her forehead before they covered her with the sheet

"Er . . . uh . . . ," The two men stated simultaneously muttered while backing up in preparation to run like hell.

"I see both of you dying in a highway accident as you return to town. A Kachina, black semi with a black crow mural on its trailer, will hit you. Might I suggest you take the back way into town? If you take the main highway, you will not live to see another Arizona sun wink its morning eyes at you."

"Back road . . . ," the two paramedics muttered simultaneously with perspiration now running down their faces. No one in either of their families had seen a real live Kachina before.

"Release me from this gurney and I will ask the Kachina Crows not to pick at your bones which will be scattered all over the main highway, should you choose to go that way."

"She can't be alive." The older Native American paramedic sputtered in a whisper to the other." She was stabbed repeatedly and bled out before she died. Her jugular vein was slit in to."

"Take a look at my cut throat if you want to, boys. There is nothing wrong with it now. I, Rio Rosa the Witch, have healed myself." Moon Dance replied in a sarcastic, eerie, wailing voice. She was trying to convince them she was a Native American folk lore Kachina.

"Undo her strap!" The younger Native American paramedic demanded the other paramedic while he stood visibly trembling. "My grandmother Raven told me all about the Kachina when I was a little boy. They will steal your soul and your children, if you give them a chance. I haven't had any children yet and I would really like to keep my manhood and sperm."

"I am not touching that gurney!" The older Native American paramedic replied. "Do you see her third eye looking at us? She did not have that third eye when we covered her up. I am Catholic. She has to be a demon or worse. If I unstrap her, she may try to possess me. My priest is a damn alcoholic. I doubt if he has enough in with God to cast a devil out of me. He can't kick his alcohol habit."

Moon Dance wanted to snicker. The two reminded her of members of her former tribe in the New Mexico desert. Some of them were skittish and spooked easily. She missed her tribe and wished that at least one had stayed behind with her. She was all alone. Benson was gone, as was Tall Willow. If they had entered deceased baby bodies to survive, it might be years before she saw them again.

"Suppose we give her a pair of our medical scissors. She could use one hand to cut the gurney strap. That would buy us enough time to jump in the ambulance and get out of here." The younger paramedic suggested.

"If we give you a pair of scissors to free yourself, will you let us live to see another sunrise" The older paramedic asked keeping his distance. "We mean you no harm, we like witches and Kachina."

"I will grant you both long life, at least a dozen children, and will let you both keep your manhood." She replied batting her third eye at the two of them, "If you give me scissors so that I can cut the straps that bind me."

"Could you limit the children you will give me to three? I can't afford a dozen on my salary." The older paramedic asked. He knew his wife at home was pregnant and he suddenly had visions of it being quadruplets. He already had two children, and medical bills out the yang from the two of them. Both of his children were cursed with a blood disorder and were constantly in and out of the hospital.

"Three it is," Moon Dance replied in a spooky sounding voice. Then, finding their reaction funny, she added, "Both of you will name your nest child after me."

"You want me to name my next child Rosa?" The father of two and one on the way asked with big eyes.

"Yes . . . I wish you to name it Rosa."

"What if it is a boy?" He asked in shock.

"You will still name it Rosa. If you do not do so, I will track you down and wither your manhood till it looks like a stick of dried beef Jerky. Then, I will steal your children's souls and rattle their bloody bones."

"She gets the scissors." The older paramedic stated removing a pair from a black medical, emergency response kit that was still on the ground and had not been loaded yet. He carefully edged his way up to the gurney and tossed the scissors next to her. Then he ran backwards towards the ambulance's door, stumbling as he did so. His friend quickly helped him to his feet and they wasted no time getting in the ambulance and speeding off.

Moon Dance took one hand and picked up the scissors. Then she quickly cut thru the gurney strap, sat up, and discarded the sheet. She then sat and snickered in amusement. She was sure that she had given the two paramedics a moment they would never forget. Amused with herself, she climbed down off of the gurney to face her new life as Rio Rosa, the risen Kachina witch.

CHAPTER FIVE

Dante

Three months had passed. Jack Benson had not returned, nor had Tall Willow. Moon Dance feared that both had ceased to be from lack of host bodies to travel in. With sadness of heart, Moon Dance settled into her new life as Rio Rosa the Kachina witch Tarot reader. From each client coming and going over the months, she inquired whether they had heard any stories concerning individuals with purple skin. Moon Dance knew that she had to find a Plutonian alien in order to be able to use their light port to go home. She was thankful Tall Willow had told her where his light port was before he left her. However, she was desperate to find a purple skinned Plutonian to activate its control panels. The lavender skin pigment was like a key or a fingerprint code. She was Weelo and had blue pigment in her skin. Only purple pigment would allow you access to the port and activate its controls. The Plutonian light ports were like private elevator shafts of light. Purple skin pigment was the keys to them.

Moon Dance, now Rosa, had experienced no contact with her former family, the crazy ranchers. She assumed that Rio Rosa had been right about Night Hawk. He had not come down to the Rio to make up with her. Apparently, Millie the eight months pregnant waitress had been more important to him than Rosa. Had Rosa not been murdered, she would be living a new life somewhere down the Rio and Night Hawk just a bad memory to her. Instead, Rosa's travel trailer remained in its setting and Moon Dance continued her life, reading the Tarot and rattling chicken bones to feed her-self.

Over the first three months, she trained her steady stream of clients into calling her Rosa Moon Dance; telling them her last name was Moon Dance. Little by little, she was being called by her own name. Only really old repeat clients still called her Rosa. Word spread after the paramedic encounter with her healing Rosa's body. Everyone along the Rio came for readings to get a glimpse of a witch who had her throat cut and then healed it. Business was good.

It was spring time on the Rio and the cottonwood outside of Rosa's travel trailer was bursting with life. Moon Dance had settled into her new life and had made a lot of new friends, mostly humans who were interested in asking questions about health issues and their love life. An old Mexican man, a border crosser about seventy, had managed to swim the Rio. Moon Dance rescued him on her side of the bank on the Rio Grande. He became her companion after she nursed him for a couple of weeks. The cold water of the Rio had caused him to take pneumonia. The swim had zapped him of some of his strength. She was lonely and needed him. He had been equally as lonely on the other side of the Rio and needed her.

Upon his arrival, Rosa Moon Dance introduced him to everyone as her father. No one questioned it. He said his name was Dante. Moon Dance asked Dante why he had risked his life swimming across the Rio, once he was well enough to talk. He told her that his wife and children were dead and that he had no one. Living across the Rio in a hut, he had watched her day to day activities as she lived in her silver travel trailer. After three months of waving at each other across the Rio, he had decided she was all he had and he wanted to die on her side of the river and have someone to mourn him. Moon Dance was pleased to have someone care about her. Dante became her right arm. She became Dante's family. Biological ties do not necessarily make people family. Love does.

Rosa Moon Dance, from day one, set down the guide lines for their life together. He did exactly as she said and Moon Dance was pleased. In return, she pampered the old man. He was seventy-six and she was twenty-four in human body years. Dante kept their little yard by the river immaculate and spent his mornings fishing on the bank of the Rio. They ate a lot of fish, frog legs, and turtles that he caught. However, Dante wasn't too excited about rattlesnake meat. In respect for him, Rosa Moon Dance didn't serve it too often, only when they were short of meat to eat.

Dante was tall for being Hispanic. He was close to six foot. Moon Dance felt safe with him sitting outside of her silver travel trailer when clients came to call. He always sat down with a machete lying at his feet. No one messed with him or her. No one left without paying either. He became the collector.

It was late spring when Dante stuck his head in the travel trailer door stating, "Rosa Moon Dance, you have a visitor. It is a man and he wishes to speak with you underneath the cotton wood. He says his name is Night Hawk."

Instantly, Moon Dance cringed. She wasn't excited about having a confrontation with Rosa's former lover and Sleeping Moon's brother. She had had her fill of the rancher brother's pranks when she was living in Sleeping Moon's host body and on their ranch. Their craziness and pranks had been partly why she had chosen to abandon their sister's body and start over. Charlie Elkhorn, their cook, had been equally as hurtful and obnoxious.

"Tell him I will be there is just a moment or so. I have to put my third eye on." She replied pointing to the scar in the middle of her body's forehead.

"I will tell him. Wear your green third eye, the emerald one. It is spring and a good day to wear green." Dante stated smiling, just before he left the travel trailer door.

Moon Dance quickly put a spot of denture paste on her host body forehead and stuck a huge fake green jewel in the middle. She held it snug for a moment or so till it was secure. Then she reluctantly left her travel trailer home and headed for the cottonwood tree.

As she neared the cotton wood, she didn't smile, but watched as Night Hawk turned and eyed her intensely. Moon Dance could tell he was nervous. She was nervous, knowing that Rio Rosa had been in a relationship with him, a hot and steamy one before her demise.

"What do you want Night Hawk?" Moon Dance asked in a not so pleasant voice. "You have a wife and a child. There is no reason for you being here."

"I . . . I need your help Rosa." He blurted out.

"That is a laugh. Go home and get your help from Millie. You were dipping into her till of help while using me. Get your sorry ass off of my property and don't return. It will be a cold day in Kachina hell that I would ever consider helping you with anything. Get lost." Moon Dance stated harshly trying to get rid of him.

"Just listen to me, Rosa. Hear me out. I don't have anyone else to turn to. Millie has disappeared."

"Couldn't keep her satisfied?" Moon Dance asked digging him.

"I want to know if you have had anything to do with her disappearance. She had nightmares about you and talked about you in her sleep before she disappeared. I have a three month old baby with no mother to see to it. You are the only person I know that has a reason to possibly hurt her."

"You are one unbelievable, conceited asshole. You think I was so hung up on you that I might have done something to your Millie?" Rosa Moon Dance asked in a huff. "If your drunken barfly, Millie, is missing; it is probably because she got tired of your cheating ass and walked away. My opinion is; more power to her. She probably saw you for the cheat you are and moved on. I don't give a damn about your three month old baby or what happens to it. Get lost and don't come back here."

"Please, Rosa. I need to find her. Everyone in town says you are the real Mc-Coy, a Kachina. I want to know where Millie is. I can't take care of the baby alone and run the ranch. Song Bird is too old to help me and the baby's crying is driving Charlie Elkhorn crazy. Something is wrong with the baby. I need Millie to come home. Please help me. The baby may die. It has all sorts of things wrong with it. On one of its feet it has three big toes. The baby is deformed and sick."

"Three big toes . . . ?" Moon Dance asked in a shock voice recalling how one of her tribe, named Three Toes, had three big toes on one foot. Was there a possibility that Millie had been pregnant by Three Toes somehow and not night Hawk? Had she tricked Night Hawk into thinking the child she carried was his. She was sure that Three Toes had gone home on the Great Mother Ship, Noah II. It was possibly that Millie had been pregnant by him and left behind. If that was so, the baby that Night Hawk thought was his was actually a half breed; half human and half Weelo.

"I wouldn't help you if you, if my life depended on it. Get lost Night Hawk. You made your bed, one of many, lie in it. I have moved on and am seeing someone else. I am not going to rock my boat by missing you and Millie into the pot. "

"You are seeing someone?" Night Hawk asked with his face flushing.

"I have been seeing someone for several months, if it is any of your business."

"Who?" He asked with a shocked look on his face.

Moon Dance could see that he was jealous. This was her chance. She would pay Rio Rosa for the use of her discarded body.

"Hasn't White Eagle told you? We have been dating for over a year. I used to meet him every Saturday night in town at the Rio Inn, if it is any of your business. I told you I was reading cards on those Saturday nights." She lied. "I was glad when Millie jumped in your bed and solved our problem. White Eagle and I plan to marry when the hype of your marriage and baby all calms down."

When Moon Dance lived on the ranch, White Eagle often spoke often of the secret lady friend he met on Saturday nights at the Rio Inn. Now she was using that bit of information to strike a vengeful blow for Rio Rosa.

Suddenly, Night Hawk had a really hurt look on his face. Was it possible that he had been actually in love with Rosa, but married Millie?

"How could you do that to me, seeing my brother?" He asked with a total look of shock on his face. "I am going to kill the sucker!" He sputtered.

"You have no right to speak of killing your brother. You had a pregnant lover back then. You were a woman user. Millie and I weren't the only ones in your bed. I wised up and moved on. Might I say, White Eagle is better in bed than you ever thought about being! Saturday nights at the Rio with him were and are like

Heaven. You were mediocre, at best."

"You don't mean that . . . "He stated with a hurt expression in his eyes.

Moon Dance had never considered that Night Hawk might actually be in love with Rosa and their affair had been hot and steamy before Millie's interference.

"I do mean it. I regret ever crawling in bed with you. It is White Eagle that I want to be with. When he asks me to marry him, I am saying yes. Get used to the idea, you egotistical fool. Go home to your child and wait for Millie, your choice, to return. She will when she runs out of money for booze or drugs."

"I . . . love you Rosa. You can't mean what you are saying to me. Millie is a mistake that I am paying dearly for. We didn't have a permanent commitment back at the time I was seeing both of you. It is me that loves you, not White Eagle. If he was in love with you, he would have told me about the two of you long ago. You have to be Rio Inn one night stands to him." He sputtered reaching out and trying to take hold of her and draw her to him.

Rosa Moon Dance immediately yelled, "Dante . . . !"

The old man came running with his freshly sharpened machete and stuck it to Night Hawk's throat.

"Touch her young rattler and your head will not sit on your shoulders."

Night Hawk immediately backed up. He could see a killer in the eyes of Rosa's new, elderly, body guard. Fear gripped him. He could see that the older Mexican man with piercing, menacing eyes was willing to die for her. He could try to pull his handgun from the waist of his jeans, but he would lose his head or arm for doing so. He backed off and put his hands up with his palms toward the old man in an 'I am backing up' demeanor. He had a very sick child to rear who had already lost its mother.

"Just tell me where Millie is?" Night Hawk demanded while keeping an eye on Dante. "Use your gift, Rosa. My child deserves to know what has happened to her mother. I need to know. Please! The baby needs her."

"If you want to find your drunk of a wife, check in town at the bars. I don't have to use my gift to know who and what she is. As far as your baby, I could care less. You slept with Millie, now you take care of the little bastard. I want nothing to do with you or the child ever."

"Rosa . . . , please help me. I have been trying to get up enough nerve for months to come and make things right with you. If it makes any difference to you, my marriage has been pure hell." He stated searching for words. "I want a divorce from Millie."

"Take your egotistical song and dance and get out of here. White Eagle and I are happy together and we intend to marry." She spit out in defense of Rosa. She was rattling a few chicken bones quite nicely. Night Hawk was visibly squirming and sputtering.

"You can't marry White Eagle. It is me that is in love with you!" Night Hawk spit out. "I'm swallowing my pride to tell you so."

"You can take your love, pride, Millie, your child, and your song and dance and stick them where the Rio doesn't flow. Now get out of here and never come back." Moon Dance yelled harshly as Dante stood next to her with his machete raised.

Moon Dance was pleased in a way and sad in a way. She had done as Rosa wanted in exchange for the use of her body. At the same time, she saw a hurt in Night Hawk's eyes and was sure that he actually was in love with Rosa. She wondered how Millie had got so mixed up in their relationship. Then she thought of her own love, Gray Feather. He had chosen a Millie type over her. Maybe all human men were cheating ass holes. Maybe Night Hawk and Gray Feather were alike. It appeared that way.

"Shall I slice off one of his arms or ears to let him know you mean business?" Dante asked in a threatening voice keeping his machete raised.

"Let the ass hole live to raise his bastard child and put up with his cheating wife." Moon Dance replied. "He deserves his marital hell."

Night Hawk stared at her and then ran for his pickup and reluctantly left.

"Thanks Dante! I just rattled a few chicken bones for an old friend. She will be happy when she shows up again."

"I like the way you rattle chicken bones, Miss Rosa Moon Dance; especially when I get to eat the chicken fried before you do the rattling."

"You catch and clean me a chicken and we will have it for dinner." Moon Dance stated smiling and then hugging his elderly arm to her. "Thank you for rescuing me."

"You are all I have, Rosa Moon Dance. "Without you, I am all alone on this planet."

"Without you, Dante, I have no one either."

"You rattle bones good, Miss Rosa Moon Dance. You had the young asshole squirming." Dante then added.

"You rattle a pretty mean machete, Dante. I think it is you that had the asshole squirming." She replied.

Dante, who was way taller than Moon Dance, smiled and hugged her shoulders. Moon Dance looked up at him. For the first time, she noticed that his brown eyes had a slight lavender tint to them. She thought that was odd, but didn't give it any further thought.

CHAPTER SIX

The Dream Catcher's Voice

After eating their fill of fried chicken, Dante retired for the evening. He slept by the front door of the travel trailer on a rug on the floor. Moon Dance retreated to the one bedroom of the trailer and after showering and putting on one of Rosa's night gowns, she climbed up into the middle of the built in travel trailer bed to think. She had some hard decisions to make. She wondered if she should hook onto the travel trailer with Rosa's fifty year old green Chevy truck and move on down the Rio, possibly setting up a new camp in New Mexico or Texas.

Moon Dance was sure it was just a matter of time till Night Hawk or White Eagle confronted her again. She wasn't sure how long she could carry off the Rio Rosa personality before someone became suspicious. She had a year to put in till Tall Willow's light port in the top of the barn, on the ranch she had abandoned, opened. She preferred to live it in peace and without the interference of the two baggage brothers from her previous life, Night Hawk and White Eagle. Also, she had Dante's safety to think about it.

Moon Dance knew that her two former brothers carried handguns and used them when necessary. They were anti-border crossers and had captured and held many for law enforcement over the years. She feared that the brothers might pull their guns and put a hole thru Dante, if he banished his machete at them again. Dante was more important to her than White Eagle or Night Hawk. He was her new family and faithful companion. She would die for him, just as he would her.

As Moon Dance was sitting there thinking, she noticed that the feathers hanging from a dream catcher on Rio Rosa's wall were fluttering, like a slight breeze off the Rio was rushing thru them. The feathers on the bottom of the dream catcher were moving and fluttering to one side. As she watched, she recalled how she and Jack Benson had shrunk themselves several months back as they entered a dream state. They had floated thru the holes in the web of Sleeping Moon's Dream Catcher and traveled in the land of dreams and nightmares to planet Weelo where they peeped at Gray Feather, Hissing Cat, and three black haired babies. Although it had been a mystical experience for her, it had not been a pleasant one.

While on Planet Weelo in the dream state, she discovered that Gray Feather had three children by someone else. The discovery nearly broke her heart. She was still in love with him. Up to that point she still fantasized that it was really her that he loved and would one day wake up and see that. That survival fantasy had been shattered. He had wasted no time sleeping with some new woman and having three babies by her. On the way back from that dream state experience, she tore out her Weelo heart and gave the shattered pieces of it to the web. Exiting the web, she no longer had the ability to love with her emotions.

Jack Benson abandoning her was another event that she could not explain. He also had declared his love for her and was intent on becoming her permanent companion. He even wanted to marry her. The last time she saw him was when he was standing behind her in the dream port as they were returning from the dream state experience. He motioned for her to go first. She did so and gave her heart to the web, not looking back. She floated thru the web, reentered Sleeping Moon's sleeping human body, and instantly fell asleep in it. Jack Benson was behind her. She had to assume he also returned thru the web and entered the host body that lay next to Sleeping Moon's. When she awoke the next morning, Jack Benson and his host body were nowhere to be found. There was no other explanation than he had changed his mind about her and had risen and walked away from the ranch before she awoke.

Moon Dance raised her hand and held her fingers in front of the open window of the travel trailer in an effort to feel the breeze off of the Rio that was causing the feathers of the dream catcher to flutter. There was no breeze. As she did, she thought she heard the voice of a child calling her. Also, it was not the voice of just any child. It was Carol Sue, Pansy Skywalker's daughter. The tiny voice seemed to be coming from behind the web of the dream catcher.

"Why would Carol Sue be in the land of dreams and nightmares?" She asked herself and then dismissed the thought. The child had gone home with the rest of her tribe to planet Weelo on the Great Mother Ship, Noah II.

Moon quickly recalled how Pansy Skywalker had flaunted her pregnancy by Gray Feather and then refused to be a mother and care for the little girl once she was born. As medicine woman for her previous New Mexico tribe, she had been forced to take the infant and raise it. Each time she fed and rocked the baby, she had the fact that Gray Feather had slept with Pansy rubbed in her face. Pansy Skywalker had been the one doing the rubbing.

"I am up here . . . Lady with the third eye. "The soft, tiny voice yelled. "Can you hear and see me? My name is Carol Sue and I am caged in the port beyond your dream catcher gate. Help me!"

Moon Dance wondered why Carol Sue would be confined to the dream port. To be there, she had to be out of her body which had to be in a dream state back on Planet Weelo. She eyed the dream catcher from her seated position on the bed and considered the fact that she might be asleep and dreaming.

"Go away little girl that I am dreaming about. I do not wish who your father's betrayal of me rubbed in my face once more. Go away!"

"I have no father or mother here. Please help me." The little voice begged once more. "Help me get thru this gate and I will be very good and go home to my Mama Moon Dance in the New Mexico desert."

"You have a Mama Moon Dance?" Rio Rosa Moon Dance asked in shock.

"Yes, she is in the New Mexico desert catching Rattlesnakes for dinner. I want to go home to her. I was treated mean on the Great Ship and put in a cage like I was a zoo animal. I want to go home to my Mama Moon Dance and be rocked by her. I miss her."

"I hear you, small voice who says your name is Carol Sue. My name is Rio Rosa. You must go away, I cannot help you." Moon Dance replied in an unsympathetic voice. She wanted nothing to do with Pansy Skywalker or her child, which was Gray Feathers. She had stayed behind on Earth to be rid of them and what they stood for. She was thru with that part of her life and didn't feel a willingness to love any of them again."

"You are not Rio Rosa. I recognize your voice." Carol Sue yelled in a whimper. "You are my mama Moon Dance. Help me!"

Then Moon Dance bit her lip as she listened to the sobs of the child she had once mothered. Carol Sue was about to have a meltdown beyond the dream catcher in the land of dreams and nightmares. The child needed her. Moon Dance had mixed emotions about rescuing her. She was Gray Feather's daughter, his love child by another. She had given her heart away to the web to be free of her nightmares and that included this child. Why would a laughing Kachina return this child to her? Should she leave her to her fate in the land of dreams and nightmares? Moon Dance questioned her-self. She had no heart to have feelings for the child she once mothered in the desert of New Mexico.

The moral side of Moon Dance won out. She lay back on the bed and silenced her thoughts. She then counted backwards as she entered that moment between awake and asleep. As she counted backwards, her Weelo body inside of Rio Rosa's physical body began to shrink. She then popped in a shrunken state from the flesh of Rio Rosa and floated up toward the dream catcher, being the size of a very small gnat.

Reaching the web of the dream catcher, she watched all the hands waving and hitting at Carol Sue denying her entrance to the Earth Realm from the in-between worlds.

"Do not fight the hands, Carol Sue. Stay back from them." Moon Dance stated seeing that the hands were slapping and hitting at the little girl who was in a filmy, blue soul state with a hint of pink in her skin color.

Moon Dance thought her coloring was odd. Pansy Sky walker was a half breed who would be half human pink and half Weelo blue. Carol Sue, if she belonged to pink skinned Gray Feather, should have skin that was three quarters pink with a blue tint, just the opposite of what she was. Carol Sue having almost totally blue skin was not a possibility.

"To get to this side thru the web gate, Carol Sue, you must choose a square section of the web that the hands are not guarding closely. Shoot thru the web and I will catch you on this side." Moon Dance stated trying to calm and direct the child who was at the point of being traumatized by the experience.

"I am scared, Mama Moon Dance." Carol Sue stated thru whimpers and sniffling. "The hands are mean. Please come get me. I need you."

It was at that point that Moon Dance realized she was going to have to travel thru the web to rescue Carol Sue. At the same time, she realized that Carol Sue had no host body to enter in the Earth Realm. The child would only have twenty-four hours to find a host body and live again in the Earth Realm with her. Children's corpses were not easy to come by. There was every possibility that Carol Sue could cease to be in the Earth Realm. In the land of dreams and nightmares she was safe. Moon Dance hesitated for a moment in thought and then decided if Carol Sue died on the Earth realm side, at least she would be in her arms. She was the mother that Carol Sue remembered and was bonded to.

"Carol Sue, quit crying and listen to me. I need you to answer a couple of questions before I come thru the web to get you."

"Hurry, Mama Moon Dance. I am scared." She stated with tears rolling down her blue, spirit being cheeks.

"Is there anyone with you on your side of the web, someone who has been watching out for you?"

"I am all alone, Mama Moon Dance. I was sent to the slaughter house. The cannibals ate my flesh. I felt myself falling asleep on the hook they had me on. I felt a sharp stun and I popped from my body and spun out of control into a swirling light and I ended up here. I threw up a couple of times from all of the violent twisting, and turning when I entered this port. Please help me, Mama Moon Dance. I am all alone here and I am frightened."

"What do you mean that Cannibals ate you?" Moon Dance inquired.

"Weelo has only one thing to eat and that is human flesh. There are no plants or wild animals there." The girl whimpered. "Pansy Skywalker was taken before me and eaten as was Hissing Cat and the girl who tended her on Earth. We did not go home to a hero welcome, Mama Moon Dance. We were all instantly penned and caged like they do cattle, sheep, hogs, or dogs on earth. One by one, we were taken, slaughtered, and our flesh eaten. Almost all of our tribe has been eaten by Weelo cannibals. Planet Weelo is not the lovely planet you told me about when you rocked me to sleep in the desert of New Mexico. It is like a dusty dry rock."

"What about Gray Feather and his friend Ralph long legs? Were they eaten?" Moon Dance asked biting her lip. She no longer had a heart to love Gray Feather, but she had memories of loving him.

"Gray Feather was in the zoo the last time I saw him. His friend Ralph Long Legs and his three children are also there. Gray Feather tends to three black haired babies who belong to some human woman who is crazy and caged next to him. I think she once mentioned she was from Arizona. Her mind has been lost to her."

Moon Dance wanted to inquire as to whether the three babies were Gray Feather's and the crazy woman's. She bit her lip and refrained from asking...

"You realize, Carol Sue, you will have to enter a human child's body on this side of the dream catcher in order to survive. I am surviving in a body that once belonged to a Tarot Reader. A rattlesnake killed the human body I was living in that you remember. Mama Moon Dance's human body that you knew died the day you all entered the space flyer to fly up to the Great Mother Ship, Noah II. My voice you know, but my body is a stranger to you."

"It is okay, Mama Moon Dance, if you are not as beautiful as you were back when we lived in the New Mexico desert. I will understand." Carol Sue stated sniffling.

"You thought I was beautiful?" Moon Dance asked in shock. "I was a seventy year old, elderly, wrinkled, Indian medicine woman"

"My Mama Moon Dance was the prettiest of all the Weelo mamas." Carol Sue added thru her tears. "You loved me."

"You do know that Pansy Skywalker is your true mother, don't you?" Moon Dance asked in response.

"I am told that, but I don't ever remember her rocking me to sleep or holding me close. You are my mama. You are the one who loved me and made me feel better when I was sick. You told me stories and made sure I had food to eat. I have no memories of Pansy Skywalker ever doing anything for me."

"If I help you travel thru the web to this side, will you do just as I say?"

"Yes, Mama Moon Dance. I will be a good girl. Come get me."

Choosing a square hole in the dream catcher's web, Moon Dance floated thru and the hands allowed it. Immediately, Carol Sue flew into her arms and Moon Dance held Carol Sue close.

"Everything is going to be alright, Carol Sue. Mama Moon Dance has come for you.

As Moon Dance held Carol Sue, comforting her, she thought about the three dark haired babies that she and Jack Benson had peeped at several months before. She wondered if they had now been eaten by Cannibals on Weelo. Were they lost in the port frightened and alone? The thought appalled her, but she did not have a heart or feelings to search for them. Also, she did not have time to look for them. Carol Sue just had twenty-four hours to find a host body or she would cease to be. She would decide later whether to return and try to rescue the three babies. Once upon a time she always put her tribe first. She was now making the decision to put herself and Carol Sue first. Carol Sue had never done anything to disrespect her. Carol Sue loved her.

"Take my hand, Carol Sue. When I say go, we will dart thru one of the squares of the web. I am going to throw something for the hands to reach for. It will distract them and give us an opportunity to escape the land of dreams and nightmares. Do you understand?"

"Yes, mama Moon Dance." Carol Sue stated as she ceased to cry. In the brief moment, she looked up at Moon Dance and gave her one of those childish smiles that warm parents' hearts.

"I need something to toss." Moon Dance muttered looking about.

"Take this . . . Mama Moon Dance. It was loose when they hung me on the slaughter house hook. Somehow, it made its way into the port with me." Carol Sue stated handing Moon Dance a small tooth. "The hands can have it. I know that there is not a tooth fairy."

"Moon Dance took the tiny tooth and turned it over in the palm of her spirit hand. "I am sorry I was not there to celebrate the loss of your first tooth."

"You are here now." Carol Sue replied sweetly. "You are my mama Moon Dance and I will love you forever."

Moon Dance wanted to tell her that she would love her forever too. However, the words just would not spill from her mouth. She had no heart to cause the words to spring forth. In the moment, she wondered if she had made a mistake giving the hands of the dream catcher the shattered pieces of her heart. Carol Sue needed her love.

"Are you ready, Carol Sue?"

"I am ready, Mama Moon Dance."

"Go!" Moon Dance shouted as she threw the tooth in the air in the opposite direction from the square of the web she intended to drag Carol Sue thru. It worked. All the hands reached for the tooth. In one quick dart and swoosh, Moon Dance and Carol Sue shot thru their chosen hole in dream catcher's web.

Laughing, the pair lay down on Rio Rosa's bed, counted forward together, and became normal size. Moon Dance let Rio Rosa's human body sleep. She needed to go with Carol Sue to hunt for a host body.

"We must be quiet and let Dante sleep while we leave this trailer and hunt for you a host body."

"Who is Dante?" Carol Sue asked staying close to Moon Dance.

"Till now, we were a tribe of two. I guess you might say he is our new medicine man, like Gray Feather once was. He will be the one who takes care of us, provides for us, and sees that we are safe. You must always do as he says, no matter what. If anyone asks, he is your father. Do you understand?"

"I understand, Mama Moon Dance. Ralph Long Legs was my temporary father on planet Weelo. He loved me. Will Dante love me?"

"Dante will love you, because he loves me."

With that said Moon Dance and Carol Sue floated thru the camper trailer wall and shot off into the stormy night sky of Arizona looking for a host child's body.

Before morning, they found one; an unexpected one.

Millie's deformed baby had died in its crib. Moon Dance with Carol Sue swooshed thru the open window of the baby's nursery. In the room's crib, a tiny pink and purple skinned baby lay dead. Its human spirit had already left it.

Moon Dance helped Carol Sue to enter the dead baby's body and then zipped her up in it.

"You must stay here, till I come for you. I will look for another human child's body that no one will miss that is your age. When I find one, I will return for you. For now, I have to return to my travel trailer and enter my host body. Do you understand?" Moon Dance asked as Carol Sue peeped out at her thru the eyes of the three or four month old severely deformed human baby. "Blink your eyes at me, if you understand."

Suddenly, the tiny baby batted its eyes at Moon Dance several times. Then it smiled one of those little gassy, burping smiles that babies have.

"I will come back for you as soon as I can work it out." Moon Dance stated. "I am sorry that the baby's body is so very ill. Be a good girl and survive in it till I find you another host body." Then with a swoosh, Moon Dance exited the ranch house and shot across the night sky returning to the silver travel trailer where Dànte lay on the floor sleeping by the front door with his machete by his side.

Moon Dance then re-entered Rio Rosa's body and fell asleep.

CHAPTER SEVEN

White Eagle Calls

A couple of days passed. Moon Dance relaxed into her new life. Night Hawk had not tried to contact her any further. She was happy about that and felt that she had paid her debt to Rio Rosa for the use of her body. Her main concern now was Carol Sue. She needed to find an appropriate aged, discarded human body to host her. An adult body would not do. She didn't have the maturity to live in one. Also, the body had to be one that no one would miss. Carol Sue, being part Weelo, needed to be raised by her and not a human family out there somewhere.

About seven in the evening, Moon Dance was preparing to read the Tarot Cards for those making their way to Rio Rosa's camp. She had a small table set up underneath the cottonwood tree. Above it from one of the limbs, Dante had hung a dream catcher and the feathers hanging from the bottom of it were flitting in the breeze coming off of the Rio. Moon Dance enjoyed reading outside as well as the variety of clients that sought her out. In spite of the fact that she and Dante was now a tribe of two, she was lonely for female companionship as well as missing the tribe of pure Weelo men who once dwelled with her in the remote desert of New Mexico, before the Great Mother Ship, Noah II, returned and rescued them. Carol Sue was the only member of her former tribe that now existed, as far as she knew.

As she was shuffling the Tarot Cards while seated and lost in thought down by the Rio, Dante interrupted her wandering of the mind.

"There is a man up by the travel trailer that wishes to speak with you." Dante stated pointing. "Do you wish to speak with him? He is not one of your clients and he is not asking for a reading. He says he is a friend of yours. I do not trust him. He looks like the Night Hawk I took my machete to."

Moon Dance turned to eye where Dante was pointing. She bit her lip knowing she was probably in for a not so pleasant confrontation. It was White Eagle and she had lied telling that they had been seeing each other at the Rio Inn.

"Send him down, but stay close with your machete. I do not know whether to trust him either. He is the Night Hawk's brother."

Dante returned to the parking in front of the travel trailer and pointed for White Eagle to make his way down to the cottonwood where she was now standing after placing the Tarot Cards down on the table. As he neared, she saw that he was smiling. That she did not understand. An angry man did not go to meet his foe with a smile on his face.

"Good Evening, White Eagle. Have you come to inquire of the Tarot?" Moon Dance asked, not knowing how to wade into conversation with him. He had been her brother when she lived on the ranch in his host sister's body. She was now living in Night Hawk's lover's body, Rio Rosa.

White Eagle walked up to her, grabbed her, picked her up, and swung her around in a circle while laughing. Then he set her feet back down on the earth and released her.

"May I ask why you are in such a good mood? In my thinking, you should probably be angry with me."

"I have pulled a lot of pranks on my brother over the years, but this is the best ever. I wish I had thought of it myself. He is currently steaming hot under the collar and not speaking to me. For once in my life, I am the man. I have come to tell you thanks for your tale of hot and heavy between us. He was a fool for letting you get away and now I am getting to prank or dig him about it. In the process, I am coming across as lover of the year. It doesn't get any better than that."

"I am glad you are taking my deception so well." Moon Dance replied. "He was seeing Millie as well as me and I never knew. She was seven or so months pregnant and he was seeing me. He used me and now I am getting even. He has the wife from Hell and I am sticking it to him."

"He deserves it, Rosa. In the meantime, I am going to enjoy my new status as the man on the ranch. I have come to ask you for a favor."

"Since you are not angry with me, I probably owe you one. What do you need?"

"Would you consider an invitation to dinner out at the ranch, on my arm, and a chance to push all of my brothers and grandmother's buttons? Because of my thick lens glasses and hearing aid in one ear, women have never found me as attractive as Night Hawk. My Saturday nights at the Rio Inn with a secret lady friend has been a lie on my part. I actually spend my Saturday nights playing poker because of the lack of a lady friend."

"I see . . . !" Moon Dance stated feeling empathy for her former brother. "I always thought that Millie was your girl; anyway that is what Night Hawk always told me."

"Millie and I dated when we were fifteen and in high school. Night Hawk stole her from me when she was sixteen. For that I am most grateful. She has become alcoholic, white trash who lives for the next bottle. Night Hawk did me a favor, although I would never tell him so."

"Rubbing me in their faces is probably not a good thing, White Eagle. Song Bird has never liked me and Night Hawk . . . well . . . he is just Night Hawk and territorial. Why would you want to rile the two of them? You are your grandmother's favored grandson and Night Hawk is your brother."

"This wild tale of you and I being lovers is the best prank that has come my way in years. As I have said, it makes me the man."

"Song Bird and Night Hawk are just likely to throw their steaks and baked potatoes at me. Are you going to protect me from them?"

"You won't need any protection. It will be me that has to run for the border. I want to announce that you and I are engaged, just to see them squirm. Song Bird signed her ranch over to me secretly, yesterday. Night Hawk can't get a divorce from a woman he can't find. Also, he now has a mistake child that he knows you will never accept. This is the greatest prank ever, Rosa. My hat is off to you. I want you to pretend to be my fiancé for the next few months or however long we want to keep up the pretense. We both get something out of the prank. I will be the man and you will get even with Night Hawk and Song Bird for their disrespect of you. You don't have to sleep with me or anything. A short kiss now and then in their presence should be sufficient to keeping their buttons pushed."

"You do know that I was in love with Night Hawk." Moon Dance stated trying to say what she thought Rio Rosa would want said. I plan to move on down the Rio Soon and start over and find someone and fall in love again. Night Hawk burned me. I want to live in a place where there is peace and not bad memories. Having a child by and marrying Millie was the lowest form of disrespect. He made me feel like I was less than white trash."

"I have always felt that I was less of a man than him because he took Millie from me, not that I want anything to do with her now. I was fifteen and made to feel like I was nothing."

"I guess we do share some need for revenge. I will do it, provided I do not have to enter-act with Night Hawk's child by Millie. I do not wish to ever see the baby seated in a high chair at the dining table on any Saturday night I come for dinner." Moon Dance replied knowing that Carol Sue was in that body and she might not be able to carry off the vengeful Rio Rosa witch part if she were present. She wanted Carol Sue to love her as the loving Mama Moon Dance she had once been.

"That is agreeable." White Eagle stated all smiles while reaching out and taking her hand in his.

"How is Song Bird?" Moon Dance asked remembering the grandmother that she had become friends with before discarding White Eagle's sister's body and leaving the ranch.

"Do you recall that hand from the Mason ranch named Tall Willow?"

"I seem to recall Night Hawk telling me that you drove him home naked once in the back of a horse trailer. As I recall, you brothers did not want your grandmother seeing him." Moon Dance replied.

"Grandmother Song Bird has half gone crazy concerning him. His body was found out in the desert along with that of Sleeping Moon. She thinks the hummers killed them. Their bodies were gutted down the front. I personally think wild animals attacked them. They had been chewed on and gnawed on extensively by the time we found them. Song Bird has been in a deep state of mourning since then and yesterday signed over her ranch to me. I wouldn't put it past her committing suicide. I don't think Night Hawk or I realized how deep her feelings were for Tall Willow. The funny thing is, Sleeping Moon's death didn't seem to have an overwhelming effect on her. She has accepted her death stating it was long in coming. I think she has always expected my sister to die and had already dealt with it."

"We all have our things we have to deal with, White Eagle."

"My sister and her lover being killed by wild animals were totally unexpected. We have no way of explaining why Sleeping Moon went into the desert with Tall Willow. Song Bird says she knows, but won't offer anything further. She has retreated into a dark hole of silence, as has Charlie Elkhorn. Then Millie happened and life just isn't what it used to be on the ranch. Song Bird gave me the ranch to keep Millie and her child from laying claim after she dies. Night Hawk is going to be furious when he finds out. She is giving him just the old camper out back of the barn. She told me that she thought Millie would dump his ass once she found out that was all he had."

"Life, as we once knew it, has definitely changed. I loved and lost. Apparently, Song Bird has done the same." Moon Dance stated thinking of Gray Feather. She still had the memories, but the feelings were gone. When she gave her heart to the web, her feelings good and bad toward Gray Feather vanished. Now, all she had was memories and coldness inside.

"Don't be surprised if Song Bird goes on and on about Kachina and demons entering men's bodies. I think her mind is slipping. Charlie Elkhorn doesn't help matters any. He goes along with her fantasies. I think she has him believing that Kachina devils are residing on the ranch. Both now make references to the fact that they fell in love with Kachina. I think his mind has slipped a little to. You would have to be around them for a few days to see what I mean."

"Sometimes people's minds play tricks on them." Moon Dance replied trying not to say too much. "Tell me about Night Hawk's baby. Why do you keep saying it is expected to die?"

"The doctors say it is deformed inside and out. Its fingernails are always this strange color of purple and it cries all the time and refuses to nurse. Over the last couple of days, it has broken out in a funny looking rash made up of blue and purple dots. The pediatrician says he doesn't know what is causing it and for us to prepare for the worse because there is nothing he can do. The baby will die. We just don't know when. Night Hawk has walked the floors with it for three months. Millie has abandoned it. Nurses take one look at it, work one day, and never return. The baby pees purple urine. "

Moon Dance bit her lip. Was it possible that Night Hawk's child was a Plutonian? If so, who was the father? It couldn't be Night Hawk because he was human. Had Millie tricked Night Hawk into marrying her? Worse yet, she had to find Carol Sue another host body. The blue and purple dot rash could be an allergic reaction. The Plutonian baby body was rejecting Carol Sue's Weelo blue gene.

"I know the baby will be a loss to all of you. However, you will have to understand that I will not let myself be concerned with the woman or child that Night Hawk dumped me for. I will not cry for the child if it dies." Moon Dance replied in a harsh voice to keep up the wicked, Rio Rosa witch image.

"I don't have a problem with that, Rosa. Night Hawked crapped on you. He deserves the bed he has chosen to lay in. So, are we on for Saturday night?" White Eagle asked.

"Pick me up at six. I wish to be back here at my trailer by eight so I can read for my clients. It is how I support myself, in case you have forgotten."

"I will pay you for your time, Rosa. That is the least I can do for you making me the man."

"The least you can do for me is to tell Night Hawk how good the sex is between us." Moon Dance added thinking of Rio Rosa and her betrayal.

White Eagle laughed. "I am the man. I will see you Saturday. Wear something that is slinky with a low neck that is appropriate to be proposed to in. I think I will kneel between steak and desert and ask you to marry me. Do you want a ring with a single stone or one of those gaudy ones with lots of diamonds?"

"Make it gaudy, White Eagle. You can buy one of those cheap big ones from a discount store. They will never know the difference."

"No . . . , you are worth the real thing for making me the man and you can even keep it after we break it off when you move on down the Rio. Expect me to present you with a ring that will dazzle them."

"You are okay, White Eagle. I will make sure I squeal, say yes, and throw my arms around your neck like you are the only man I will ever love. Don't be surprised if I throw in a passionate kiss. Just don't gag. I know I am not your type." Moon Dance stated trying to think and act like Rio Rosa.

"You are guaranteed that I am going to passionately kiss you back. Don't you gag! I know that it is Night Hawk that you are hung up on. You can slip into my bathroom afterward and use my mouth wash if you want."

With that said, White Eagle hugged Moon Dance and left whistling.

Dante made his way down to the bank of the Rio where Moon Dance had her table set up underneath the cottonwood tree.

"He was laughing and you were smiling, so I didn't interfere. Is everything okay, Rosa Moon Dance?"

"Have you ever heard of a white, Native American, or Mexican baby that had a rash composed of purple and blue dots?" Moon Dance asked to try to make sense of whether Night Hawk's baby had a rash or was having a possible reaction. She hated to think that Tall Willow was possibly the father of Millie's baby. She didn't know of any other Plutonian living in the area. Anyway, Tall Willow had not mentioned any during their short friendship after they left the ranch and leaving their human bodies behind. Had Tall Willow been using Song Bird and didn't love her as he indicated? Or, was there another Plutonian living and breathing in the vicinity of the ranch, possibly a rapist? If there was, he was capable of activating and running the Plutonian light portal on the third floor of the Seven Moons Ranch barn. Millie had to of been raped by a Plutonian and then she tricked Night Hawk into believing the baby was his. In Moon Dance's thinking, Millie had reason not to want to rear the baby and running away. Perhaps she heard the humming like Song Bird did.

"Yes . . . I have heard of babies with blue and purple dot rashes. Mexican folk lore says they are children of the gods born into human bodies that try to reject them. They are possessed with Kachina or devils. In Mexican folk lore the babies with dots always die. Purple gods and blue gods are not compatible." Dante stated.

"You have answered my question, Dante. Thank you."

After her discussion with Dante, Moon Dance resumed her identity as Rio Rosa and read the Tarot cards for a steady stream of clients till almost midnight. Dante lit a candle on the table when night was falling for her to read by. He seemed to always know what she needed and when.

CHAPTER EIGHT

The Storm's Gift

As Moon Dance, now Rio Rosa Moon Dance, completed her readings for the evening, the sky above the Rio Grande turned dark and threatening. Dante, sensing a fierce storm was brewing, helped her quickly remove her reading table from the bank of the Rio. The Cottonwood tree was starting to bend in the wind. After hitching the travel trailer to the back of Rosa's old green pickup truck, they prepared to move inland and to higher ground. Fighting a spitting rain, got in the pickup cab and rolled up the windows.

"We must hurry and make our way to higher ground, Rosa Moon Dance. The washes will fill with water and the bank of the Rio where we now sit will be covered with flood water. Those are devil clouds rolling across the sky above us. They will soon drop rainfall by the buckets. All will be washed away here within the hour. This night may become one of the living dead." Dante stated as he started the pickup up.

As they were about to pull out, Moon Dance spotted flashlights across the Rio on the Mexico side.

"Surely they are not going to try to swim across the river with the sky about to turn on like a flood!" Moon Dance stated pointing for Dante to look across to where a small group of individuals, carrying totes and bags, were wading into the edge of the water of the Rio Grande.

"Desperate times cause desperate people to try to beat the odds, Rosa Moon Dance. I was desperately lonely the night I swam the river home to you." He stated as he shifted gears, getting ready to drive them to higher ground.

"We can't just leave them here, Dante." Moon Dance stated in a panic seeing that some of the individuals were children.

"I will return for them, Rosa Moon Dance. However, I cannot help them till they reach this side. I will return to the bank of the Rio, after I get you safely to higher ground."

Moon Dance reached over and put her hand on top of Dante's which was on the steering wheel. "Maybe they are new members of our family swimming home to me. You swam home to me. My arms long for a child to rock."

Dante turned his face toward her and then grinned strangely as lightning started striking fiercely outside of the pickup cab. He then sped out and they moved the trailer a quarter of a mile inland, away from the Rio. Then He insisted Moon Dance stay behind and put on a pot of coffee, stating those he would bring to higher ground would be cold, wet, and needing to warm themselves. He then left her and returned to the Rio in the pickup to rescue those trying to cross.

After getting the coffee maker going, Moon Dance went to the rear of the travel trailer where she slept to get blankets to warm whoever Dante brought back with him. Seeing that the feathers on Rio Rosa's dream catcher were fluttering; she wondered what was causing it. All the windows of the travel trailer were closed. Was there some sort of storm brewing on the other side of the dream catcher, beyond the hands, in the land of dreams and nightmares? Moon Dance reclined on her bed to watch the movement of the feathers as she waited for Dante to return. She hadn't intended to doze, but she slipped into a half sleep and half awake state. That is when she heard a voice calling her.

"Woman with Third Eye . . . help me!"

Popping from the sleeping human body of Rosa, she floated up to the dream catcher and peeped thru.

"Who are you and why are you calling my name?" She asked.

"Well, if this isn't my lucky day. I once found Gray Feather in the desert and now I have found you!" A shocked voice behind the web exclaimed."I recognize your voice."

"You know me?" Moon Dance asked trying to peep thru the web and its many hands that were guarding it.

"It is me, Pansy Skywalker." The voice replied. "I have returned to you and I need your help to get thru the dream catcher's web."

"You cannot be Pansy Skywalker! She went home to Planet Weelo. Go away and let me sleep." Moon Dance huffed. "Ruffle someone else's dream catcher feathers."

"It is definitely me, Pansy Skywalker. You watched Gray Feather and I make love on the sand dune back in New Mexico. Does that convince you that I am who

I say I am?" The voice replied.

"What was the result of my seeing you on the sand dune?" Moon Dance asked wanting to know for sure that it was Pansy.

"I dumped my unwanted child by Gray Feather in your lap nine months later." Pansy replied. "I need you to help me get thru the web. There are others from your tribe here with me. Help us! The hands of the web keep throwing us back on this side when we try to reenter Earth's realm."

"The hands guard the web for good reasons. They keep Kachina, from other planets, from entering the Earth's realm. You must be a Kachina or the hands would grant you entrance." Moon Dance replied remembering how the hands of the web had tried to keep her from re-entering Sleeping Moon's bedroom in her last human incarnation.

"Carol Sue is here in the port with us. You love her! She is not evil. I would hold her up for you to see, but she is wandering around somewhere. I can't find her at the moment. She wants to return home to you, her mama Moon Dance."

"Who is with you besides Carol Sue?" Moon Dance asked, trying to decide if it truly was Pansy Skywalker. She knew that she had already rescued Carol Sue from the web. She now lived in the baby's body that once housed Night Hawk and Millie's little Kachina.

"Hissing Cat, Honey Bee, and many other Weelo I do not know are here. Help us, Moon Dance. The hands of the web won't let us cross over to your side of the web. We want to return to Earth, your side of the dream catcher."

"Why would you want to return here? You were very happy to board the ship and leave me in the desert to die alone. I do not need any more of your disrespect."

Then, a second voice from beyond the web joined in on the conversation.

"It is me, Hissing Cat. I am sorry for taking your Gray Feather. Please help me, Moon Dance. My body is gone and I am doomed to float about as a spirit being in this unreal place of nightmares and dreams. I am sorry I disrespected you and took Gray Feather for myself. I have paid for my crime against you. I was slaughtered like a pig, eaten, and my soul sent into this dream port hell."

"Is Gray Feather with you?" Moon Dance reluctantly asked.

"He is paying for his crime against you, just as we have done. He is caged naked like an animal and sits in a zoo for all to stare at."

"He sits naked and on display in a zoo?" Moon Dance asked repeating Hissing Cats words

"Please help us return to Earth and your side of the dream catcher. I will do anything if you will help me." Hissing Cat replied ignoring Moon Dance's question.

"Why is Gray Feather in a zoo? He is a doctor, a scientist like me." Moon Dance asked stirring the conversation in the direction she wanted it to go.

"We did not return to a planet that welcomed us with open arms. We were all immediately sentenced and punished for not letting you, the captain of your space flyer, board first. All of us had forgotten that boarding before you was a punishable crime on Planet Weelo. Those of us here in the port have paid by being sent to a slaughter house where we were killed and butchered for meat. Planet Weelo is no longer made up of a population of vegetarians. They have turned to cannibalism. Also, there are not but about a dozen or so men on the planet. Women rule. Gray Feather has been put on display as a male specimen for Weelo women to gawk and stare at. Many of the younger women of the planet have never seen a male. Gray Feather and his friend Ralph are side show attractions in the zoo." Hissing Cat replied.

"Please help us cross over, Moon Dance. Slap the hands of the web; do something! "Pansy Skywalker yelled interrupting the conversation.

"I helped all of you survive for years in the desert. I hunted rattlesnakes to feed you and wet your brows with cold water when you were ill. I rocked and fed babies that were not mine. I sat up with the sick and the dying. It did not matter what I did to insure the survival of all of us, you betrayed me and took the one thing I loved the most, Gray Feather. I never asked for anything from any of you. You have reaped for the disrespect that you dished out to me. I will not help any of you. I have no reason to." Moon Dance huffed.

"Do it for Carol Sue! You love her!" Pansy begged, not realizing that her child had already been rescued by Moon Dance.

"Because I do care for Carol Sue, I am leaving you all where you are." Moon Dance replied. "I will raise her to respect those who rock, comfort, and feed her."

The sound of Hissing Cat sobbing floated thru the veil. "Please, Moon Dance, if not me or Pansy, will you help Honey Bee and the other women of our tribe make their way back to you? They are not guilty of taking Gray Feather from you. Help them!"

"Have a heart you old witch!" Pansy Skywalker yelled angrily interrupting Hissing Cat.

"I have no heart!" Moon dance yelled back in a huff. "That is why I am now telling all of you to go to Weelo Hell. I once loved all of you enough to let you go home in spite of your disrespect. Live with your choices. "

As Hissing Cat sobbed and Pansy Skywalker cursed beyond the web, Moon Dance floated back down and re-entered the sleeping body of Rio Rosa. Rousing from her dazed, sleep state, Rosa Moon Dance rose, removed the dream catcher from the trailer wall, carried it into the tiny kitchen of the travel trailer, and then placed the dream catcher portal door and its trailing feathers in a huge ash tray. Then she set it afire, using a lighter left behind by Rio Rosa who smoked.

"This dream catcher, a border crossing gate between worlds, is now permanently closed to Weelo immigration."

Then, Moon Dance, watched as the web and the feathers disintegrated in flames. When the web was fully afire, she opened the trailer door to let the smoke and stench out. When the web was consumed, she took the ash tray to the door and threw them out as though they meant nothing to her. She did not have a heart to love them or feel sympathy for their plight.

Moon Dance listened to the lightning and thunder making its powerful presence known outside the travel trailer as she waited for Dante to return. The coffee was brewed and she had quilts ready to wrap and warm anyone he had managed to rescue. She had saved Dante's life when he swam the Rio to her. Now, he was returning the favor to someone else.

Dante was a kind old man, in spite of the fact that he had lavender tinted eyes that screamed he had secrets locked within him. Moon Dance was not able to figure out what his secrets were. It was as though he feared sharing whatever was locked up inside of him. She didn't pry. There were skeletons in her own closet that she didn't want rattled.

About an hour passed and the storm outside was fierce. Moon Dance was starting to get extremely nervous. Dante had been gone way to long. A couple of hours elapsed. Starting to pace the tiny hallway floor in the travel trailer, she was relieved to hear the pickup pull in with Dante honking its horn. She hurried to the trailer door and flung it open. She could see, from the illumination of repetitive, fierce lightning striking, that Dante was pulling someone from the passenger side of Rio Rosa's pickup. As he neared her, she could tell that it was a drenched child that lay limp in his arms. Moon Dance held the travel trailer door open and he carried her inside and lay her down on the floor on the rug he slept on.

"All perished Rosa Moon Dance. Only this one floated to our side and I fear she is now dead also." He stated as he knelt and closed the little girl's brown eyes. The drenched child corpse was that of possibly a six or seven year old girl.

Moon Dance knelt beside him and pushed back the black hair of the little girl which lay in wet ringlets stuck to her face. She had short hair like a boy. Moon Dance told herself that the little girl's hair may have been cut to get rid of head lice. Looking closely, she did see some nits. Running her hand over the child's hair, she emitted Weelo rays and killed the lice eggs that were there. She had powers that she didn't use often, especially in front of humans. They called everything evil that they did not understand.

"I could not save her, Rosa Moon Dance. She died in the pickup on her way home to you. I am sorry. A child would have been a good thing for me and you to love." Dante stated as tears rolled out of his eyes. The others, her family and friends, did not make it to the bank on this side of the Rio. They were swept downstream by sudden flooding from the washes."

Moon Dance instantly thought of Carol Sue who needed this human child's discarded body. The sick, deformed, baby body belonging to Millie was a temporary host and a way too confining tight fit. This discarded Hispanic child's body was Carol Sue's size and answer for survival on Earth. Moon Dance knew that Dante would never tell where the Hispanic child came from .They could rear Carol Sue as their child. She was pleased.

Thinking quickly, Moon Dance replied to Dante as she lowered her face and rested her chin next to the child's nose to see if she was breathing. She was not. Moon Dance then felt beneath her jaw on her throat for a pulse. There was none. The human child was indeed dead and its human spirit had taken flight.

"The child is not dead, Dante. She just deep sleeps." Moon Dance stated picking her up. "I will take her to my bed and warm her. There is coffee on the cabinet. Dry yourself off, warm yourself with those blankets, and guard us against the storm till it passes. Move us further inland if necessary. I will care for our child and revive her. If it is alright with you, I will name her Carol Sue. My last client for the evening was named Carol Sue." She stated lying. "I liked her name."

"You will give her my last name, Rosa Moon Dance and I will father her well. She will be called Carol Sue Dante. I will love and protect you and her till I take my last breath on Earth."

"You will never know how much you mean to me, Dante. Thank you for our child." Moon Dance replied and then headed for the one bed room in the back of the trailer. After closing the bedroom's little door, she laid the dead Hispanic child's corpse on the bed and covered it up.

Then, in a flash, exiting Rio Rosa's body, Moon Dance shot thru the trailer wall in her blue, filmy, spirit being form and then flashed across the stormy sky toward White Eagle's ranch to get Carol Sue out of Millie's deformed, baby's body. She would then return with the spirit being of Carol Sue and her into the little Hispanic girl's dead, discarded body. She had to do it quickly, before Dante got curious and discovered Rio Rosa's human body on the bedroom floor and that the Hispanic child was not alive, but actually a corpse. She feared that Dante, should he discover her secret, would call her a demon like Charlie Elkhorn had once done months before. She did not want Dante to run from her. She needed him to fill her lonely hours. As a rule, since Gray Feather, she did not let herself have human friends. They could not be trusted. She had befriended and learned to care about Dante. She had no heart to love him. Respect was the nearest thing she had to give him. Dante had earned that part of her.

CHAPTER NINE

Bodies In The Desert

Charlie Elkhorn stood at the center island in White Eagle's ranch house. He was preparing steaks for the evening meal. Lying next to his wooden cutting board was a loaded revolver. Since his discovery that a demon had been walking around in Sleeping Moon's dead body, pretending to be her, he was taking every precautious measure to protect him-self. Next to the revolver, set a tiny vial of holy water from the church. Charlie Elkhorn was Catholic, even though he was Native American.

As Charlie Elkhorn prepared the steaks, he tried to ignore the crying of Millie's baby. It lay down the hall in a crib in sleeping Moon's old bedroom which was now a nursery. The infant never stopped crying. It didn't matter who tried to comfort it, the baby cried non-stop, 24 hours a day. Suddenly, the crying stopped. Charlie laid down the knife he was using and listened for a moment. The crying did not resume. He wondered if perhaps, the baby had finally let go of Earth life. The infant's death had been anticipated ever since it was born.

Charlie feared that the severely deformed baby, both mentally and physically, had been entered and possessed by the blue Kachina demon spirit that he saw discarding Sleeping Moon's body. He never entered the baby's nursery or held the child in fear of that. His life had become a nightmare since he discovered that the woman he was in love with was a demon. Charlie now feared every bump in the night. Worse was the fact that he could not tell Night Hawk and White Eagle about his experience in fear of them thinking he had going insane. He needed his job as the ranch cook for the present. Secretly, he had been applying to other ranches in the north for a cook's position. His priest had advised him to move on secretly so that the demon did not follow him.

Song Bird, grandmother of White Eagle and Night Hawk, entered the kitchen. "I need you to give me the pea shooter that you and the boys have hidden from me." She demanded holding out her hand with the palm up. "The baby has quit crying. I fear the hummers have come to possess it body or yours and mine."

Charlie looked at her and saw that she was sharing his nightmare. "You know about the blue Kachina?" He asked almost in a whisper with perspiration beads breaking out on his forehead."

"Have you seen them . . . the humming Kachina?" Grandmother asked in shock. "Everyone has told me all my life that I am crazy because I say I have seen one. I am old and my eyes are not young. However, Charlie, the Kachina demon I saw had purple skin. It tried to seduce me and take me into the other world with it. I fought it and ran. "

"The Kachina may have many colors of skin, grandmother. Humans have many skin colors. We are red Native Americans. Our ranch foreman is white and the horse breaker is black. I believe you, Song Bird."

"Thank you, Charlie. May I have my pea shooter? The baby has ceased to cry. I am afraid to go into the nursery without it."

"Let us put our ears to the baby monitor by the table first and listen for breathing." He stated picking up the vial of holy water in one hand and his revolver in his other."

"I am afraid to go listen at the monitor. The demon might make its way thru the monitor and enter me thru my ear, Charlie Elkhorn. Give me my handgun."

Frightened him-self, Charlie stuck his revolver in the waist of his belted jeans. He then walked over to the cabinets above the stove, opened a door, reached way back in, and pulled out the grandmother's antique pea shooter. Then he removed the revolver from the waist of his jeans and made the sign of the cross with it in his hand.

"Charlie, I am old. If the demon tries to take me, he is not going to get much. My doctor says my heart is getting worse and I may die within the next year or so. I will listen to the baby monitor first."

I will listen, Grandmother Son Bird." He stated walking over to the baby monitor that hung on the wall behind the chair that Night Hawk usually sat in. There were no sounds of a baby breathing.

"The baby is silent, Grandmother." Charlie stated handing her the small handgun that belonged to her. "I will go for Night Hawk so that he can close his child's eyes in death. He is shoeing horses. Stay here in the kitchen where you are safe. It is Night Hawk's rite to go in first."

"Hurry and bring him back, Charlie! I am sure the hummers are here." Grandmother Song Bird demanded in a frightened voice. "Night Hawk will believe us if he enters and sees the demon Kachina."

"Take this. It is holy water from the church. The priest gave it to me to ward off demons and devils. Un-cork the vial and throw it on the Kachina; if you are approached by one."

Then, with his knees feeling like jelly, Charlie Elkhorn quickly exited the ranch house to go get the baby's father, Night Hawk. He was positive the baby was dead, although he had not looked.

~   ~   ~

Moon Dance, in blue filmy form, floated next to the crib of Millie's deformed, Down syndrome baby. It was a pathetic looking little body with deformed limbs and covered with a blue and purple spotted rash.

"Mama Moon Dance . . . is that you?" Carol Sue asked in a small voice from within the baby's body. She had been crying, but ceased when she opened the baby's half blind eyes and saw a blue filmy form.

"It is I, Carol Sue. Now be quiet while I get you out of that baby's body. I have found you the discarded body of a little Hispanic girl to live in. She is your age."

"Thank you Mama Moon Dance! I have cried ever since you left me here. This baby's body is too tight for me. Every time one of those rancher people picked me up, this body would pinch me in different places. I have had to scream bloody murder to get them to put me back in this crib."

"You will be okay now, Carol Sue. The girl's body is in Rio Rosa's trailer. You will be able to live with me and Dante down by the Rio now. I will be your mother and Dante will be your father. We will be a family, a Hispanic human family to all we come in contact with."

"Hurry and let me out, Mama Moon Dance. The baby's body has places that itch that is driving me crazy. The baby's body does not like me." Carol Sue wailed.

"I think that is because the baby's body has plutonian genes. Human bodies, we are compatible with. Plutonian bodies, we are not. The baby has a rash, an allergic reaction to your blue gene. Keep quiet while I unzip the baby's body and get you out."

The room became eerily quiet. Moon Dance took one finger of her blue filmy hand and ran it down the baby's body from the top of its head to the crotch area. The body opened like it had been unzipped like a zipper in a dress. Instantly, Carol Sue sat up and then popped out of the baby. She then floated next to Moon

Dance and hugged and nuzzled her.

"We cannot leave this unzipped body here, Carol Sue. Grandmother Song Bird is afraid of hummers. That is what she calls us. She and Charlie Elkhorn have seen unzipped bodies. It is best if they think someone has kidnapped the baby. We need to keep our presence on Earth a secret in order to survive."

"I understand, Mama Moon Dance." Carol Sue replied just happy to be out of the baby corpse body.

"We will take the body and bury it in the desert." Moon Dance whispered.

Then Moon Dance heard footsteps in the hallway outside of the room. She picked up the baby's corpse just as Grandmother Song Bird flung open the door and stepped into the room, frightened out of her gourd, with the vial of holy water uncorked in one hand and her pea shooter in the other. The elderly woman in her eighties fired her pea shooter and then threw the holy water at the filmy blue spirit being of Moon Dance. Then the old woman fainted, thinking she had confronted a pair of Kachina demons.

"Hurry Carol Sue, the others won't be far behind her."

Then Moon Dance pointed to the open window of the room. Carol Sue floated thru first and then Moon Dance followed in a flash carrying the limp, unzipped corpse of Millie's baby. Then in an attempt to hide from any further discovery, Moon Dance took Carol Sue by the hand and they shot out into the desert taking the baby with them. The sky was still menacing and looked like it could drop more buckets of water on the desert at any time.

After flying about five miles out into the desert, they stopped. Moon Dance looked behind them to see if they were being followed. She didn't see vehicle headlights or hear the sound of horse hoofs. Only the sounds of thunder and the flashes of lightning were trailing them.

"We will bury the child's body here, Carol Sue." Moon Dance replied still looking back in the direction from which they had come.

"Who are all of those humans sleeping down there on the desert floor with no shelter from the storm, Mama Moon Dance?" Carol Sue asked pointing downward as lightning flashed illuminating the landscape.

"Humans . . . ?" Moon Dance questioned turning her attention to Carol Sue and where she was pointing. More lightning flashed making the spot and the bodies lying there visible.

Moon Dance knew in an instant that she was viewing a group of dead bodies, possibly border crossers.

"We will not wake them. They are probably border crossers, Carol Sue. Humans are superstitious. They will think that we are Kachina or devils should we wake them. We will fly further into the desert to bury this baby's body."

With that said, Moon Dance and Carol sue flashed another five miles out into the desert and left the deformed baby beneath a cactus, after covering its tiny body with sand. There was not time for last rites, the offering of prayers and good-byes.

Moon Dance took Carol Sue by the hand and then flashed across the rainy, stormy, eerie night and returned to Rio Rosa's trailer. There they shot thru the bedroom wall and landed on the bed next to the corpse of the dead Hispanic girl who lay covered up. Moon Dance then quietly helped Carol Sue into the six year old Hispanic girl's dead body and zipped her up. Moon Dance then re-entered Rio Rosa's body and sat with Carol Sue till adjusted to her new human body and then fell asleep.

An hour later, Moon Dance exited the trailer's bedroom to join Dante and have a cup of the fresh hot coffee she had made earlier for him. He was pleased to have her join him and proceeded to pour both of them a cup of the black steaming brew. Together, they took their mugs of coffee to the door of the travel trailer which they opened. Then they stood watching the lightning flashing and listening to the thunder that sounded like the beats on war drums.

CHAPTER TEN

Elkhorn's Medicine Bag

Aweek had passed since Moon Dance and Carol Sue had buried the body of Millie's deformed baby in the desert. Carol Sue, now a six year old Hispanic, adjusted quickly to her new life as the young daughter of Rio Rosa the Tarot reader and Dante her companion. At night, she had nightmares about Planet Weelo, the slaughter house, and her body being eaten by the cannibals there. Of a day time, she was a normal child who chased lizards and frogs along the banks of the Rio and played house with a wooden doll and carved dishes that Dante made her. To all outward appearances, she was a normal child. Only the night frightened her.

From noon to midnight, Moon Dance read the Tarot for anyone showing up to support the three of them. Dante was too old to work, plus he didn't have a green card. Moon Dance used Rio Rosa's driver's license for ID. Dante and Carol Sue stayed out of sight if anyone questionable appeared for a reading. Border crossing patrols often stopped asking if any illegal crossers had been seen. Moon Dance always produced Rio Rosa's Id and told them no. Rio Rosa, as it turned out, owned the ten acres on the banks of the Rio that her travel trailer sat on. Apparently, she had won it in a poker game from a rancher that owned all of the land around it. That was a surprise to Moon Dance. Apparently, Rio Rosa had been a cigar smoking, witch of a Tarot reader who liked an occasional poker game.

Over the months, Moon Dance turned down several invitations to secret card games with high stakes by Rosa's clients. Moon Dance wondered if Night Hawk had been aware of Rosa's obsession with poker. After giving it some thought, she was sure that he did. Night Hawk had held his share of poker nights in the old travel trailer out back of the barn on his and White Eagle's ranch. Maybe, that was where Rosa learned to play. That part of Rio Rosa's life was not pursued by Moon Dance. Poker was not her thing, survival on Earth was.

About two weeks after Carol Sue came to live with them, Moon Dance had a surprise visitor. She was a little flabbergasted when she walked down to the river bank and saw who was seated in the late evening shadows beneath the cotton-wood tree, smoking a cigar, and waiting for her. It was Charlie Elkhorn, the cook who had declared his love for her, when she was in Sleeping Moon's body, and then backed off and called her a demon when she unzipped the ranch girl's body and showed him who she really was. Moon Dance bit her lip and reminded herself that she was now Rio Rosa, not Sleeping Moon.

"You have come for a Tarot reading from Rosa?" Moon Dance asked unsure of how to approach him. She wasn't sure what his and Rio Rosa's relationship was. Night Hawk was his Charlie Elkhorn's boss and he had probably served and cooked numerous meals for Rosa.

Charlie raised his eyebrows as though something was wrong. "When did you learn to mimic Sleeping Moon's voice, Rosa?"

"If I sound like her, I sound like her." Moon Dance replied trying to dismiss the subject. "She was teaching me to speak more properly just before she passed on."

"That is a laugh, Rosa. She hated your guts. She hated anyone that was prettier than her. Now cut the crap. Sleeping Moon is dead. It is not wise to mimic the dead, especially if you think they might come back to haunt you."

"Why are you here, Charlie?"

"Can you make medicine love bags and things like that?" He asked as he nervously lit a second cigar. He already had one on the side of the table which was smoldering and dropping ashes on the ground beside the table she read the Tarot at.

"You want me to make a medicine love bag for you?" Moon Dance asked in a shocked voice.

"Well, can you make them?" He retorted and he nervously twitched one of the two lit cigars.

"Of course I can!" Moon Dance replied lying to keep up Rio Rosa's witch image.

"If you can make them, can you also make medicine bags to protect men from demons?" He spit out and then looked at her strangely like he was afraid of something.

Moon Dance was sure that she knew what he was afraid of her. She bit her lip.

"It depends, Charlie. Do you want protection from male or female demons?

Night Hawk should have come to me for a medicine bag to protect him from bar-flies. He would not have his Millie problems if he had done so."

"This is nothing to joke about, Rosa." He huffed with a nervous far-away look in his eyes. "I . . . I fell in love with a woman and then found out that she was demon possessed. When I discovered what she was, a Weelo Kachina, I ran. I have done everything to protect myself from her returning. I got Holy Water from the priest to protect me and those living in the ranch house. The demon has possessed Night Hawk's child before it died, making it cry day and night like a banshee. Song Bird walked in on a pair of female demons as they stole Night Hawk's child. One was an adult and one was a child. I fear the female demon will come for me next. She wants me. I think she took the baby as a warning to me that she would return for me. I need a medicine bag to protect me. The holy water did not affect the demon when Grandmother Song Bird threw it on her. I am returning to the god of our fathers, the Great White Spirit, for help."

Moon Dance wanted to take Charlie Elkhorn's cigar and shove it down his throat. She was the being he had declared his love for and then run. Also, she was far from being an evil one. She dealt out five Tarot Cards slowly while she thought about what her response, as Rio Rosa, should be. Survival was more important than getting even with Charlie.

"Get over it Charlie. Grandmother Song Bird has always heard what she calls hummers. You are buying into her fantasy." Moon Dance replied trying to not sound so much like herself.

"You have not been to the ranch for some time, Rosa. We have been cursed ever since the night I saw the demon. Song Bird has gone crazy in the head. Night Hawk walked out into the desert with a loaded revolver drawn and raised. He did not return and we have not found him or the baby. I am sure they have both been taken to the blue demon's hell, wherever that might be. Only White Eagle and I remain on the ranch. The hands have all quit."

In a way, Moon Dance felt sorry for Charlie. He was actually afraid, even though he had nothing to be afraid of from her except having his cigar possibly crammed down his throat.

"What else is bothering you, Charlie, so I will know what to put in the medicine bag." Moon Dance replied.

"Only Song Bird and I have seen this blue demon woman. It does not matter that I am a grown man, Rosa, I am afraid. I think Night Hawk's mother was the first taken by the humming demon and Tall Willow and Millie were next. There have been many individuals that have come up missing in this area. There is no explanation as to what happened to them. I think there might be a portal to hell somewhere in the back desert."

"What makes you think that Charlie?" Moon Dance asked suddenly having her interest.

"Sometimes when it rains, I go to the back porch of the ranch house and stand and smoke. On several occasions, I have seen frozen lightning flashing in the back desert."

"What do you mean when you say frozen lightning?" Moon Dance asked.

"A bolt of lightning will flash touching the floor of the distant desert. Instead of disappearing then as lightning does, the bolt becomes frozen like an ice cycle. It hangs from Heaven to Earth. Only demons could make frozen shafts of light. I think the ice cycle frozen lights marks Hell's entrance. However, I am too afraid to go look. I do not want to become one of the missing."

"Night Hawk has probably killed himself in the desert with his gun. He probably lost it knowing his bed was dead and missing. His bones will one day be found. If I were guessing, Millie got tired of playing mama to a sick child and just abandoned all of you. Night Hawk's mother probably did the same as Millie." Moon Dance replied trying to ease Charlie's fears. "However, the cards do not show me that. That is my opinion."

"A family of border crossers has been found in the back desert Rosa. Demons opened them up like they had zippers after cutting their throats. I think the demons have done it. Before being committed, Song bird said Night Hawk's baby was split open from head to its crotch when she walked in on the demon woman who had it in her arm. You may be right about Millie and Night Hawk's mother, but how do you explain the family of border crossers being split open?"

Moon Dance once again bit her lip knowing that she was the blue filmy being that he called a demon. The insinuation hurt. However, she could not say anything to Charlie that would arouse his suspicions concerning her.

"Were you drinking the night you saw the demon woman?" Moon Dance asked rolling her eyes at him like he might have been drunk and hallucinating.

"I was sober, Rosa. I wasn't afterwards." He stated puffing hard on his cigar from being overly nervous. "I am at my wits end, Rosa, and scared out of my gourd. I want you to make me a medicine to wear around my neck that will ward off evil spirits. I want you to make one for White Eagle also."

"There is only one thing that will cause hell demons to run from you, Charlie Elkhorn." Moon Dance replied suddenly coming up with a solution to get rid of him.

"Lay it on me, Rosa. I have tried everything. The humming on the ranch is getting louder and more frequent. We used to laugh at Song bird because she said she head humming. Now we all hear it. The ranch hands quit as quickly as White Eagle hires them. All the old hands are gone."

"Ice and snow is the answer you seek, Charlie. Demons, as you say, come from Hell, a place heat and fire. They live and breathe it. If you want to be free of them, move to the land of ice and snow. They won't follow you there. In the land of ice and snow, they would become frozen like the shaft of lightning you speak of."

"That sounds logical, Rosa. Thanks." He stated rising to leave.

"Not a problem, Charlie! Pay Dante my $40.00 up at the trailer and have him send my next client down. Return tomorrow for the medicine bags."

After he was gone, Moon Dance wondered if the dead border crosser family in the desert was the same one she and Carol Sue had happened upon when they were taking the baby's body into the desert to dispose of it. She had not taken the time to look the deceased family over. She had been in a hurry. Was it possible that beings like her-self were hiding in the back desert? Dante said the border crossers they tried to rescue had been washed down the Rio and drowned. Was it possible that alien beings from the back desert pulled the family's bodies from the Rio, un-zipped them, and then used them as host bodies for a short spell? Did the beings dispose of them in the back desert afterward? If there were alien beings living in the back desert, there was no guarantee that they were friendly or peaceful.

After Charlie, a Hispanic woman, named Maria Martinez, walked down to the reading table beneath the cotton wood for a reading. She was a regular client and came once every two weeks when she got paid. Maria was a restaurant hostess. She ran the cash register for her brother's eating establishment. Moon Dance always enjoyed her visits to her reading table. Maria knew anything and everything about all things that was going on in town. She was a walking newspaper with many columns of details.

"What do you wish to ask the cards?" Moon Dance asked starting off their conversation after Maria was seated.

"I want to know of the cards where the missing little girl is . . . " Maria asked picking up a paper fan from the table that Moon Dance kept there for clients to fan themselves with during readings. "If I find her, I can collect the reward that is out for her."

"There is a little girl missing?" Moon Dance asked while Maria gave her damp neck a good fanning. It was a warm and muggy evening on the bank of the Rio. "Do I know her?"

"You do not know her, Rio Rosa. She was a border crosser."

"Why is there a reward out for her?" Moon Dance asked shuffling the Tarot cards.

"It is how her parents and brothers died on this side of the river that has caused her to be of interest to law enforcement. The family was just poor Hispanics hoping for a better life here, like most border crossers."

"How did they die?" Moon Dance asked laying out five Tarot cards for Maria's reading.

"They were murdered. They were cut open with a knife from the top of their heads down to their crotches." She replied picking up one of the Tarot cards to eye it." There was a mama and a papa, three teen boys, and a little girl. They could not find the little girl. Animals may have dragged or carried her bones and body into the desert."

"That is awful, Maria. "Moon Dance replied, suddenly realizing that some alien or aliens, such as her-self, had used the family of bodies as hosts. "How old was the little girl?"

"I do not know her exact age, but she was pretty young. A doll and a hair barrette were found on the ground by the bodies."

"I see . . . ," Moon Dance replied slowly in thought. "Why are you interested in the reward money?"

"If you read the cards and they tell me where she is in the desert, I will go find her, collect the reward, and buy myself a new living room suite with the money. You must see my worn out couch, Rosa. It has so many holes from my brother's cigarettes that it looks like Swiss cheese. He is financially strapped right now and is living with me. He sleeps on my couch and it is now so pitiful to look at. I am going to kick him out when I get my new suite. He can sleep on a rollaway in the garage."

"The Tarot never lies, Maria!" Moon Dance stated turning over three cards in front of her. She had gotten good at bluffing and reading into what people wanted to hear.

"What do the cards say, Rio Rosa. Will I collect the reward and get my new living room suite?"

"The cards say no. They say someone else needs the money worse than you." Moon Dance threw out.

"Damn it!" Maria replied as she stopped fanning and eyed the three cards laid out in front of her. "My brother needs money worse than me. He is two months behind on the rent for his restaurant building. Is he going to find the girl and collect the reward? If so, I am going to insist he split it with me. I could at least buy a new roll away bed."

"The cards say that it will be many years before the missing girl case is solved, Maria." Moon Dance replied hoping that Carol Sue's host body was not that of the little missing girl. Dante had said the family of border crossers he encountered had been swept downstream and drowned. It had to be a freaky coincidence that both families of border crossers had a little girl. Dante said the little girl was the only one that washed up on the U.S. side of the Rio and the only one he could rescue. That satisfied Moon Dance's mind. One family was washed up on the Mexico side. One family was found in the desert. They had to be different families.

"I had my heart set on that living room suite." Maria stated sighing and fanning a little harder.

"Do you wish to ask anything else this evening of the Tarot?"

"I guess that is all I am interested in this time. However, do you want to hear some good gossip?" Maria asked pulling a pack of cigarettes from her pocket and then lighting one in the candle that graced the reading table.

"How good is the gossip?" Moon Dance asked knowing that Maria was dying to tell her the latest dirt on someone in town.

"Don't you dare tell anyone I told you, do you promise?"

"Cross my witch's heart," Moon dance replied making a cross sign in the middle of her upper torso.

"Night Hawk and White Eagle's crazy grandmother has finally gone and lost it. They have committed her to the crazy house for old folks. She claims to have seen a demon snatching Night Hawk's sick baby. Millie's baby is missing from the ranch. Anyway, those of us who know Song Bird think she may have lost it, killed the baby, and possibly disposed of it in the desert. We also think she might have killed Millie." She stated half whispering; as if there were anyone around to hear.

"If I were guessing, Maria, Millie has probably run off with some trucker or liquor salesman that can afford to buy her a bottle or two in exchange for favors." Moon Dance replied, not wanting to get involved with the events of the ranch, since there was a baby missing from there and a little girl missing from the desert. She didn't want to draw any attention to the fact that she now had a six year old girl and a companion who had no green card. She definitely did not want to be connected to Night Hawk's missing baby.

"Just between you and me, I don't think the baby belongs to Night Hawk." Maria further added in a whisper.

"What makes you say that?" Moon Dance asked out of curiosity.

"Miss Wilson down at the drug store told me that the nurse in the emergency room told her that the after midnight Emergency room clerk told her that Millie was seen one night there claiming to have been raped by a purple man. Afterward, she denied the purple man part and convinced Night Hawk that the baby was his. I think Millie's baby belongs to that crazy guy that lives down by the rail road track who wears those crazy purple western boots. He is strange. He painted his old rusty trailer purple. Could you ask the Tarot if the baby belongs to Night Hawk or the crazy man?"

"I am too close to Night Hawk to ask such questions of the Tarot. In case you have forgotten, I was dating Night Hawk at the time." Moon Dance replied. "A witch cannot inquire of the Tarot for herself. She will lose her powers. As much as I would like the baby to belong to the crazy guy, I cannot ask."Moon Dance replied. "Night Hawk dumped me for Millie, remember?"

Maria laughed. "I am sorry, Rosa. I forgot you and Night Hawk had a thing going. I am also sorry that he turned out to be such a jerk. Who would have thought that he, with all of his money, would crawl in bed with a low life like Millie? What was he thinking?" She asked flipping her stub of a cigarette away onto the bank of the Rio.

"With his thing . . . ," Moon Dance replied and then both women snickered and laughed.

CHAPTER ELEVEN

Jack Benson Returns

Several weeks had passed since Carol Sue became a permanent member of Moon Dance and Dante's family. Moon Dance was sure that Gray Feather had probably been slaughtered and eaten on her home planet, as had all of her tribe that had left her behind in the New Mexico desert. Although she remembered her former tribe and wondered about their fates, she had no heart to care about what had happened to him. Moon Dance was now making logical and rational decisions to create a good life for her-self, Carol Sue, and Dante.

Saturday night dinner at White Eagle's ranch never materialized. On the night that Millie's sick baby disappeared and Song Bird had collapsed in the floor, Night Hawk walked out into the desert with his revolver drawn following what he thought was a kidnapper. He did not return and Song Bird was committed to a mental institution. Thus, there was no need to avenge Rosa by showing up to dinner at the ranch on White Eagle's arm. There was no one to prank. The days of pranks and brother rivalry ended.

Carol Sue, Dante, and Moon Dance settled into a pleasant life on the bank of the Rio Grande. Moon Dance home schooled Carol Sue to keep the government off of her back and social workers from calling. Dante became Moon Dance's guard and best friend. Her new life seemed perfect, except for an occasional day when Dante got a far-away look in his eyes like someone or something was calling to him. Moon Dance could not put a finger on what his problem was. On those occasions, he would wander away from their camp by the Rio for a night or two and then return, usually carrying a couple of rabbits or a small wild pig. He always told her that he had been hunting. Moon Dance never questioned him about his disappearances. She let him have his private skeleton time. She had her own closeted skeletons that she did not wish to speak of. Perhaps Dante had a female Gray Feather memory that he was running from. Maybe the night hunting was his way of dealing with whatever his secret was. She did not want to rock her boat with him, so she didn't pry.

Carol Sue quickly adjusted to her new life as the daughter of a Tarot Reader. She also speedily grew to love Dante and think of him as her father, even thought he was quite old. Dante, in human years, was seventy or more. He did not let his age get in the way of his playing with her and teaching her to fish the Rio and how to hunt and survive in the desert. Moon Dance taught her what she needed to know to survive in the human world. The first lesson was not to fall in love with a human man because they would love and leave you. This lesson, Moon Dance taught Carol Sue when Dante was not around so that he would not be offended. He was a human.

Dante was the exception to Moon Dance's rule. She had no heart to love him, but she did have respect and spoiling to give him, and that she did. She never failed to praise him for anything he did to make their lives good. She gave him all of what she did have to give him. He, somehow, seemed to understand. The one thing that fascinated Moon Dance was the lavender shade in Dante's eyes. She had heard of humans with lavender eyes, but they were rare. Also, for a Hispanic man, he was very tall. Moon Dance felt that in his younger days, he had to have been quite handsome, a lady killer as the white humans said. The age difference did not bother Moon Dance. In human years, she was in her twenties. Dante was in his seventies. What did matter was that they enjoyed each other's company.

As time passed, Moon Dance relaxed and put aside her suspicions concerning his skeletons. He was always kind and gentle to her and Carol Sue. He never raised his voice or did anything inappropriate in their presence. He was just a kind, gentle, old man and they felt lucky to have him in their lives. His affinity for night hunting, they put up with. Dante was just Dante.

Eleven months passed and it was just before noon on a sunny morning that Moon Dance was preparing for her day of Tarot Card readings. Her clientele had mushroomed with all the talk around town about demons and Kachina stalking the area. As Rio Rosa, she was making a small fortune selling medicine bags. Humans feared death. Those living in the area feared walking out into the desert and becoming one of the missing. The list of the missing in the area was growing and most of them females in their late teens and twenties. All the missing women had one thing in common. All were mothers of one child.

Moon Dance had just showered and dressed for the day. Standing before the tiny mirror in the tiny travel trailer bathroom, she concentrated on putting a dot of denture paste on Rio Rosa's forehead to secure a huge, fake, emerald jewel in place. The round green jewel made Rosa's forehead scar look like a third eye. Moon Dance had become accustomed to dressing and looking like Rosa, just as she had once been accustomed to looking like an Indian medicine woman when she lived in the desert of New Mexico. Beneath her human host bodies, she was a filmy blue, Weelo being.

Rio Rosa, the pink human spirit, had not returned to demand her discarded human body back. Tall Willow also had not returned. Her dream of going home to Planet Weelo with Tall Willow in his light port had died. She was resigned to the fact that she and Carol Sue would probably live centuries of reincarnations on Earth and in different bodies in order to survive. Her greatest sorrow was that her companion and human friend, Dante, would one day die and leave them. Human life spans were short and he was in his seventies. Moon Dance did not want to think about Dante's mortality.

Even though Carol Sue told Moon Dance nightmare tales about the slaughter house, she wasn't sure she believed the stories. Carol Sue had just been five when the event occurred and maybe she had over exaggerated it. Moon Dance did not want to accept the fact that her planet was now a society of cannibals. Planet Weelo had been a lush, green planet when Moon Dance had left it on Noah I to visit Earth to harvest specimens for her scientific research projects. Planet Weelo had been almost a utopia at that point. She just couldn't fathom the fact that her planet had spiraled downward into cannibalism. Weelo had been a planet of vegetarians when she left on the Great Mother Ship, Noah I.

Dante stuck his head into the open bathroom door where she was fiddling with the fake, emerald jewel.

"You have a visitor. I do not recognize him. He is Native American and says he has made his way here from the north. He wishes me to tell you that his name is Jack and that he was trapped on the other side of the web last year. He says he has not been able to make his way back to you till now. He is dirty and has hitchhiked a long way. He may just be a transient who wants to con you for a hand out. Do you wish to speak to him or do you wish me to send him away? I think he is a little loco." Dante stated making the crazy circling sign around his ear.

"Did you say his name was Jack?"

"He says he is a doctor named Jack, Rosa Moon Dance. In my opinion, a doctor would not wear the rags he has on."

"Send him away. I don't know anyone from the North. The only Jack I have ever known walked out on me before I met you. He was a handsome white man that slept with me one afternoon and when I awoke he was gone. My friend Jack was definitely not a Native American."

"Yes . . . Rosa Moon Dance." Dante replied. Then, he turned and left.

As she finished securing the jewel, Moon Dance replayed her memory of Jack Benson and the day they floated thru the dream catcher's web together in Sleeping Moon's bedroom. She had made it back thru the web, but fell instantly asleep afterward when she re-entered Sleeping Moon's body. When she awoke, Jack Benson, whose body slept next to her, was gone. A thought occurred to her. Was it possible that he had been trapped the other side of the web and some alien being, needing a body, had taken his that slept next to her. A body without a soul cannot get up and leave on its own accord. If the Indian man outside was truly Jack Benson and he had been trapped behind the web in his spirit state, some other spirit being had made it thru the web possibly and snatched his human body. If this were the case, she had wrongly assumed that Jack had abandoned her.

"It can't be Jack . . . ! My mind is playing tricks on me." Moon Dance in Rosa's body muttered.

Finally satisfied with the emerald's placement, Moon Dance gave into her curiosity. She would take a quick peek at the Indian man just to make sure it wasn't Jack. She owed the doctor from the Great Mother ship that much respect.

Leaving the bedroom, Moon Dance made her way to the trailer door and was about to open it when it swung open violently. The Indian man had a hold of its door knob and was struggling with Dante to gain entrance.

"Moon Dance . . . it is me Jack Benson. Call your apes off."

Rosa Moon Dance jumped back in fright. The voice sounded like Jack, but the body was not how she remembered him. Dante, being very tall, quickly overpowered him, threw him to the ground, and put his machete to his throat in a threatening manner.

"Don't kill me . . . don't kill me!" the Indian man begged as Dante eyed him in anger. "Moon Dance, help! Call of your two goons. It is me; I am just in another body."

"I am not a goon and the Jack I know abandoned me months ago." Rosa Moon Dance shot back in disgust as Dante held the stranger, named Jack, on the ground."

"Call Moon Dance to the door. She will tell you that she knows me."

"I am Moon Dance, Rosa Moon Dance. If you knew me, you would recognize me."

"You are Moon Dance?" the Indian asked and then he started laughing.

"Who are you, is the question I?" Moon Dance retorted in a huff folding her arms across her chest. Then, her light bulb went on. She was living in a new host body that Jack Benson was unfamiliar with. She was no longer in Sleeping Moon's body from the ranch. She was in Rio Rosa's body and she had dated Night Hawk.

"How did you talk Night Hawk's girl out of her body?" He asked still laughing. "She is hardly your type."

In disgust at his laughing, but realizing that he was who he said he was, Moon Dance motioned for Dante to release him.

Dante grabbed Jack Benson by the collar of his western shirt and pulled him to his feet roughly after removing his machete from his throat.

"You will swallow your sneering laugh, or you will lose your head to my machete when she is thru with you." Dante threatened as he banished his machete in front of Jack Benson's face.

"I get your meaning! " Jack Benson stated forcing himself to quit laughing at the body Moon Dance had chosen for a host one. "You have to understand, she is not the Moon Dance I remember. A fortune teller is a step down for her, more like an elevator plunging down a hundred flights."

Instantly, Dante raised his machete to take off Jack's head.

"No . . . Dante . . . !" Moon Dance yelled. "I will deal with him. He has information that I am in need of. I didn't recognize his new western look. I will speak with him beneath the cottonwood tree and then he will leave us. Keep our child inside, till then."

"Yes, Rosa Moon Dance." Dante replied lowering his machete.

Moon Dance then pointed to the cottonwood tree down on the bank of the Rio. She then escorted Jack Benson, in his new Native American host body, there to talk.

CHAPTER TWELVE

Dante's Personal Obsession

D ante had done as he was told. He had Carol Sue inside the travel trailer and was watching out the window to make sure that Rosa didn't need him to take care of the unwanted stranger. Sometimes he resented Rosa bossing him around. However, living with her was good cover for who he really was. Playing the part of the 'old peasant man that was some distant relative of Rosa' kept him off the radar screen of the border crossing guards and Arizona law enforcement. Rosa had lived in her travel trailer on the banks of the Rio for five or so years. No one questioned her presence. Everyone knew her.

Dante watched as the stranger seemed to be having a heated discussion with Rosa down beneath the cottonwood. He could not hear what was being said, but he could see that Rosa was angry and having it out with him over something. He did not leave the travel trailer but kept Carol Sue inside. He did not want to upset his applecart with Rosa. He was just fifteen miles from the back desert camp where the gathering was now taking place. Sleeping in her trailer floor was preferable to sleeping on the desert floor with those of the gathering in sleeping bags. Soon it would be time for him and the others to go home. Till then, he would continue to be Rosa Moon Dance's friend and companion. He secretly wanted to be more.

Dante recalled the day he swam across the Rio to Moon Dance's side and let her pull him from the Rio. He had been watching her for some time and was fascinated with her. Letting her think that she had rescued him had been a smart move on his part. He had wormed his way into the life of Rio Rosa, the witch that an ordinary Hispanic man couldn't touch with a ten foot pole. He was pleased with his deception and had made every effort to make her dependent on him. He needed her as a cover till the gathering took place and then the mass exodus from the desert. Rosa Moon Dance had fallen for his kind old man projected image.

What Dante had not expected, was to fall in love with her. He was jealous as he watched the man arguing with her down by the Rio. Rosa Moon Dance had never spoken of the younger man who had just arrived in dirty rags. The thought of anyone from her past reentering her life pushed all of his buttons. As jealous as he was, he could not do anything to upset his position in her life. He needed to stay with her in hiding till there was frozen lightning in the sky. At that point the gathering would enter their last phase and then disappear from the back desert.

Dante had a secret. However, he realized that Rosa Moon Dance also had some secret past that she was not speaking of. He hoped it was not the man he was watching thru Rosa Moon Dance's window. He wasn't sure he could stand back and let her take a man besides him-self to her bed. He had been fighting his desire to make love to her. He knew he absolutely could not give in to that desire and why. His secret prevented him from doing so. Also, Rosa Moon Dance was in her twenties and he was over seventy in earth years. He was sure she would aught if he undressed all of his wrinkles and approached her about crawling into her bed.

As Dante stood watching out the window of the travel trailer, he saw that Rosa seemed to be getting really upset. Feeling she might need him, he left Carol Sue in-side playing with her doll and he went outside and stood with his machete raised in case needed. He was boiling on the inside and resented the younger man that was arguing with her. Some of their words were reaching his ears when they were talking loudly. Apparently, they had slept together in her past. He was catching just bits and pieces of their conversation. The thought of Rosa Moon Dance sleep-ing with the dirty stranger that stood beneath the cottonwood tree bothered him, he wanted her for himself. He desired to be in her bed and was fighting an internal war with himself in order to stay out of it.

Dante knew that he had fallen in love with Rosa Moon Dance. However, was too old to be in her bed. Also, he had a secret, a skeleton in his closet. Even if his friend, the gorgeous Rosa Moon Dance, invited him to her bed, he could not ac-cept her invitation.

~   ~   ~

Moon Dance stood down by the Rio angry that her past was trying to interfere with her future.

"How did you find me?" Moon Dance asked knowing she left nothing behind at the ranch that indicated where she was going. She was even in a new host body.

"I was in the dream catcher portal and came across an old acquaintance of yours named Hissing Cat."

"How did she know I am now Rosa? She went home to planet Weelo long ago with my tribe."

"She was lurking in the shadows inside the dream port and watched you enter there thru the web. Some child there was calling for you to come get her. The child was calling you Mama Moon Dance. She then watched you take the child back thru the web to the Earth realm side. She tried to follow the two of you, but the hands of the web would not let her thru. She told me that Rosa the Tarot card reader was also you, Moon Dance. I was shocked for a moment to find that you had taken Night Hawk's Rosa as a host body. Were you desperate?"

"I could ask you the same thing." She retorted in annoyance. "You hardly look like a doctor."

"You have made your point." He replied wiping the smile off of his face. "Did you say that you have a child?"

"Dante and I have a child, a boy." She replied lying. "What do you want Jack? You abandoned me after we returned thru the web. I do not believe your portal story about Hissing Cat or how you managed to find me. Your human body that lay next to me was gone the next morning when I awoke after our adventure. After pledging your loyalty to me, you walked out and didn't even say goodbye. Now, tell me what you want. I do not have time or the desire to play games with you. Dante and I are companions and we have a son." She stated lying once more about the son part. She didn't want to discuss Carol Sue, nor did she want him to see Carol Sue in case he had seen photos of the missing six year old Hispanic girl. He had abandoned her. She wasn't sure that she trusted him.

"Do you love Dante?" Jack asked. He had hoped to find her waiting for him.

"I respect him. In case you have forgotten, I gave all the shattered pieces of my heart to the web when I floated thru. Love is no longer part of me. I make rational decisions now, not rash ones from the heart. I have chosen Dante and he has chosen me. We are family and we have a son."

"What about me? I thought we would one day find each other and possibly marry." He asked in an uncontrollable outburst. "You have to know that I am in love with you and always have been. That Dante creep is human. He will die. You can't step down thru the centuries with him from host bodies to host bodies. His pink spirit will fly off to his own source of being when his human body ceases to be. He is not like us. You and I are pure Weelo. It makes sense for us to be together."

"I have chosen Dante and I stand by my choice. Jack, I am happy for the first time in many years. That was not the case when I had my heart to love with. You, Gray Feather, and my tribe abandoned me with no thoughts to my welfare or emotional state. There is no room in my life now for you. I have replaced you with Dante. You must return to planet Weelo or choose a new life for yourself on Earth, as I have. I will never love again. My heart is gone. Dante is happy with just my respecting him. He is the right choice for me and we are very happy."

"I did not abandon you, Moon Dance. I got trapped beyond the dream catcher's web and was not able to follow you thru it. What happened to my host body that lay next to you in Sleeping Moon's bed, I do not know. Dante is human. He will either die or betray you some day. Humans are fickle and show no true allegiance to anyone but themselves. When the chips are down and disastrous times hit, he will run like hell. I am who you should be with!"

"Dante is faithful to me and will never leave me." She replied coldly. "You left me sleeping in Sleeping Moon's bed and wondering what had happened to you. You didn't even leave a note."

"I did not abandon you on purpose . . . !" Jack huffed. "I was trapped in the portal with our planet's dead and the humans they had slaughtered and eaten for meat. It was a nightmare place."

What Carol Sue had told her concerning cages, cannibals, and slaughter house deaths flashed across Moon Dance's memory.

"When and if you were truly trapped the other side of the dream catcher's web, did you hear any gossip or references to my tribe who went home to Weelo on the Great Mother Ship, Noah II." She asked out of curiosity.

"I spoke with many Weelo ghost beings in the land of dreams and nightmares. They are all trying to find ways to come thru the many dream catcher, web gates and find host bodies here. Hissing Cat, Pansy Skywalker, Honey Bee, and Running Deer are in the dreams and nightmares portal. I heard nothing concerning the others. However, there are so many Weelo and human ghosts there, that I could have missed seeing some of the others."

"How many ghost beings dwell in the in-between world of dreams and night-mares?"

"Thousands dwell there in the unreal realities that humans call dreams."

"As a doctor and a scientist, Jack, what do you feel is the current state of Planet Weelo? Is it stable or spiraling downward as I have been told?"

"While I was trapped beyond the web, I spoke with many of our planets past elite, professionals, and military. They all told the same story. Weelo is now a female populated planet of cannibals. Food is short and anyone not productive is sent to the slaughter House where they are put to death and then processed as meat. If you become ill or unproductive for any reason, you are seen as unnecessary and not worthy of further partaking of the planet's short food supply. Women now rule the planet and men are almost an extinct being. The only place to find a man now, on planet Weelo, is in the zoo as specimens or in the male brothels. When the couple dozen men there don't perform, they enter the food chain. The men in the brothels are humans. The Weelo women prefer them for some reason, probably because they do not have the advanced intelligence to over throw the all female governing force. Weelo men have just about been eradicated like they were cockroaches or other unwanted pests. Weelo men are just about extinct. Only those managing to make it to earth and other similar planets will survive. I met a man named Tall Willow in the portal. He was abducted by Plutonians when he entered a host human body in the back desert from here. He was housed in a zoo for a few days and then sent to the food chain, killed, and butchered. The cease to be gun mal-functioned on him and he ended up in the dreams and nightmares portal. He was sent to the slaughter house because the zoo keeper discovered that he was a Plutonian living in a host human body."

"What do you mean when you say put to death? Weelo are eternal, so are Plutonians."

"The cease-to-be gun is a new invention. Not only does it kill flesh, it also destroys the soul. The eternal soul of the Weelo and Plutonians now has an enemy and it is the cease-to-be gun. We are no longer the lion with no predators. We are now vulnerable to anyone in possession of the new weapon."

"Surely you jest, Jack Benson. I don't remember our planet heading in the direction of Cannibalism or in the direction of producing mass destruction weapons to use on our own kind. When I left Planet Weelo, we only harvested humans for zoo specimens, not for meat."

"You have been gone from Planet Weelo for thousands of years. I also have been gone that long. We were both on the Great Mother Ship, Noah I, when it crashed. There have been many changes and evolution has changed our race from plant eaters to meat eaters. Those in the land of dreams and nightmares portal tell the same story of how they ended up there. The 'cease to be' death weapon malfunctions occasionally. When it does, soul beings pop from their flesh bodies and are sucked thru a vent that has a grid on it like the dream catcher's web has. As Weelo ghosts, they then became trapped in the land beyond their grid of dreams and nightmares. They don't wish to return to Planet Weelo and look for new host bodies. There is every possibility that they would be sent again to the slaughterhouse and not be so lucky to have the gun malfunction a second time. They feel their only hope for living again is to enter Earth host bodies and reincarnate over and over and over, a never ending circle of life and Earth death of their host bodies. They are all looking for ways to exit the dream catcher's web. It is the only hope for the survival of our race."

"I am saddened for my planet's problems, but I no longer have a heart to care." Moon Dance replied.

"You and I hold the key to leading a new society of Weelo. We know how to get them thru the web and find them host bodies. Those beyond the dream catcher's web are mostly the less intelligent of our planet. We could be the father and mother of a civilization. Our knowledge of how to survive here on Earth would automatically make us the new leaders of our race. We would have the say so of who joined us here on this side of the web. We could demand loyalty and respect."

"You are delusional, Jack Benson. If we let the lower classes, the unproductive, and degenerates of our Weelo society enter here, it wouldn't be any time till their crimes would bring Earth's governments and law enforcements knocking at our door. We survive here in small numbers because we live in small tribes as hermits. The less desirable of our race would put them-selves on display and unzip their bodies for food, favors, and whatever else they could get, as long as they didn't have to be productive. Our ability to heal all Earth traumas and diseases would make us valuable. We would become slaves, bought and sold because we would not be a large enough race to defend ourselves from slave hunters." Moon Dance replied." Some of those ending up in the slaughter houses of our planet may have been for good reasons. We would be foolish to let them thru the web and welcome them with open arms. I survive here on the bank of the Rio because I am a smart Weelo woman who follows rules and keeps to herself."

"We could pick and choose who we bring thru the web." Jack Benson replied rolling his eyes. "This is our chance, Moon Dance, to be someone. When we left planet Weelo on Noah I, our small orb had rulers, a king and queen. We were pe-ons who would never have been invited to stand before them. Thanks to the cannibals on our planet now, the rulers have been done away with, eaten. It is a good thing for us. We have the opportunity to be the new King and Queen and lead a new Weelo civilization here on Earth. "

"Why don't those of intelligence in the portal pick a desolate green planet, such as Jupella, and start again? They would not have to worry about hiding and fitting in with the human race. Humans are not easy to get along with and they will turn on you at a moment's notice. They are wild animals that have not been fully civilized. They are like lions and will eat and destroy anyone crossing them."

"It is the chance of a lifetime, Moon Dance. You are not seeing the overall picture. You and I are the overall picture. We could be rulers, the elite of a new society."

"You are delusional, Jack Benson, as I said before. I will not help you. For one thing, I plan to return to Weelo and see for myself if what you say is true. If it is, I will find a way to migrate to Planet Jupella and start over there. A life on that desolate planet, with its wild animals for companions, would be preferable to living with humans here. I plan to travel to Plutonia and then make my way to Weelo from there. I have discovered a way to get there. I just have to wait for passage to be available. There are other alien beings on Earth besides us. They have advanced modes of travel, between planets, that is far superior to Weelo's antiquated Great Mother Ships. I have secretly befriended one of those aliens. He has agreed to let me be his traveling companion."

"Does your human lover, Dante, know that you plan to abandon him?" Jack Benson asked sarcastically.

"I will find a way to take Dante with me. He is my companion, not my lover." She retorted. "I will secretly take him along as my house boy, if I have to. Dante goes where I go now, and forever. If he wants to sleep in my bed, it is okay with me. What Dante wants, Dante gets . . . no questions asked. He is the one person on Earth that has loved me and respected me. He is forever with me."

"You are making a big mistake, Moon Dance. That guy with the machete is a low class peon, and hardly ruler material."

"That is your opinion, Jack Benson. It is not mine. Dante is loyal to me."

"What about his wife and kids? He is old enough to have an aging old hag of a wife and grown children that are older than you, Moon Dance. He probably has grandchildren your age. Are you nuts? I doubt seriously that he will abandon his Earth life, travel with you, and leave all behind."

"You are an idiot, Moon Dance. You should listen to your own words. I think you said that humans are like wild animals and they will turn on you when things don't go their way. Your machete man may take his weapon to you someday when you do not live up to his expectations, or his so called dead wife shows up on your doorstep."

"That will never happen, Jack Benson. Dante and I don't lie to each other. We need to trust each other and we do for both of our survivals."

"I guess I should return to the portal and ask Hissing Cat or Pansy Skywalker to rule the new race with me. I sure as hell am not getting thru to you. Both of them would jump at the chance to be a queen and rule a new Weelo civilization."

"Do what you wish Jack! However, don't bring your new tribe of misfits here to me. I have a good life with Dante and I have no intentions of helping Hissing Cat, Pansy, you, or other Weelo beings from behind the web to start a new Weelo civilization. I gave my heart away to the hands of the web after my tribe disrespected me. Hissing Cat and Pansy Skywalker were at the first to do so. My heart is gone and now I don't give a dam what happens to them or you, although I am curious as to whether Gray Feather is alive or a victim of the slaughter house. Even if he has been eaten by my Planet's cannibals, I have no heart to care. All of you and the memories of you are like a dull movie that I watch occasionally, but don't find interesting enough to get involved in."

"Isn't there anyone in our old tribe that you halfway have feelings for, or owe allegiance to?" He asked out of desperation to get her to listen to him.

"There is no one. All betrayed me and I have no heart to forgive."

"What about North Star? All she did was enter your space flyer before you. "

"You may tell me about North Star. However, I am not asking about her. I have no reason to."

"North Star has managed to keep herself out of the food chain by flying a food harvesting ship. Those providing food for the planet are safe from the slaughter house. She is now a captain."

"I see." Moon Dance replied. "Is she and Ralph still an item?

"I don't know, Moon Dance. The productive of your tribe were separated from the unproductive the minute your space flyer docked on Noah II. North Star and Ralph were separated as were all couples boarding, according to Hissing Cat. Only the elite on Planet Weelo now have the privilege of owning a man or being with one."

"That pleases me. At least Hissing Cat did not get to keep what she took from me. What happened to Pansy Skywalker? Did she take up with Gray Feather, where Hissing Cat left off?"

"There are some things I cannot tell you, Moon Dance. It is possible. I do know she was held in the zoo along with Gray Feather and Ralph for a short time. Her daughter Carol Sue was of interest to the elite class of women on the planet. I am not sure why. They may have been saving Carol Sue as some sort of reward for someone's service to the planet. In my opinion, the little girl was a type of caviar being saved for a special party or social event of the cannibals. She was slaughtered just before a big party. Pansy Skywalker went to the slaughterhouse the day after she did."

"Where did you get that information? You said Hissing Cat was slaughtered right after leaving the Great Mother Ship."

"One of the Weelo zoo keepers had a minor stroke. Like all of the other sick on the planet, she was sent into the food chain. Before going there, she had overseen the human zoo specimens. I spoke with her beyond the web in the portal. She told me about Pansy."

"What was the zookeeper's name?" Moon Dance asked casually. She really didn't trust what Jack Benson was telling her. He had abandoned her. If he gave her a name, she would travel thru the web and ask the zookeeper if he was telling the truth. She just couldn't believe that her home planet had slipped into such a depredated life style.

"I don't recall her name, Moon Dance. I talked to so many Weelo ghosts in the portal."

That figures, Moon Dance thought. He is lying to get me to leave Dante and go with him. It isn't going to work. Dante will never abandon me. He may be human, but he is faithful to me and only me.

"What can you tell me about the Weelo male population?" Moon Dance asked wanting to catch him in a lie.

"There might possibly be a dozen Weelo men left the planet and they are owned by the elite or ruling women. Men are at the bottom of the pecking order and what few remain are slaves. The elite females of the planet each own one Weelo male. Just as farmers on Earth sell off young steer because they only need one bull, the unnecessary men on our planet have been killed and sent to the slaughter house. Just as an Earth farmer butchers and puts his unwanted or unnecessary young bulls in his freezer, only the prize bulls are kept. The unnecessary steers are in the freezers or food panties of the all female population. The elite ruling class own one bull or male slave each. He services her whole family just as one bull services a farmer's whole herd."

"You are feeding me a bunch of crap, Jack Benson. One bull servicing all the women in one family would eventually, over a twenty year period, start producing deformed off spring. The bull, as you call him, would start servicing his own off-spring. You are a doctor. Don't feed me that crap. Weelo is an advanced civilization that knows better."

"I am not lying to you, Moon Dance. I am just telling you what the women in the portal have told me. "

"A planet of women overpowering a planet of males, killing them for food, and making a minor few of them slaves is not logical." Moon Dance huffed. "Not only that, what do they do, eat male babies born to them?"

"That they do, according to the zookeeper I spoke with. That fate is better for the males born than being sent to the two male brothels."

"What do you mean by saying there are two brothels of human males?"

"There are two male brothels on Weelo. In each there are twelve males. Being with a man is a reward to the loyal, productive members of the Weelo work force. Sleeping with one of them is like getting an end of the year or quarterly bonus here. The men in the two male brothels are not Weelo. They are human males that have been harvested from earth. The twenty-four men that make up the two brothels are safe from the food chain as long as they can perform and service whoever they are awarded to. If they fail to satisfy the woman they are awarded to, they enter the food chain and are replaced by another human male that has been harvested. The average male in the brothel lasts three months. The human males are sex slaves. They are shown what the one consequence is for not doing what they have been harvested for. Men on Weelo are not seen as a necessity, except for servicing the female population and the filling of their freezers."

"The women on Planet Weelo are smart to avoid relationships and use the services offered them. I should have taken Gray Feather for a sex slave, instead of an object of my heart. I could have shared him with Pansy and Hissing Cat without hard feelings existing between us." Moon Dance replied to see what his reaction was.

"Surely you don't mean that, Moon Dance. I love you. Love is not something that can be replaced by just being serviced by a man. I can't be replaced. My love for you can't be replaced." Jack replied in a disgusted voice at what she had said. "Is Dante your servicer? Is that why you keep him around?" He asked in a huff.

"Think what you want to Jack Benson. I have chosen Dante and he is what I want."

"Turn your bull, Dante, out to pasture. It is me that you should be with. We have friends and a race of people behind the web in the dream portal that we are capable of helping and ruling. We could be the new Adam and Eve and all those in the portal our slaves in a New Garden of Eden."

"I am sorry, Jack. My life is here with Dante. My tribe disrespected and discarded me like I was unwanted garbage. They didn't even think enough of me to try to bury my human remains before they entered my space flyer to return home. Dante makes me happy. If you want to call that servicing me, so be it."

"Have a heart, Moon Dance."

"I have no heart, Jack. I gave all of its shattered pieces to the hands of the web when I floated back thru Sleeping Moon's dream catcher long ago. I have no emotions or feelings now, just dull memories."

Moon Dance watched as Jack suddenly put his hand inside of his ragged, dirty, western shirt and pulled something out in his hand, concealing what was in it. Then in a fast move, that Moon Dance was not expecting, he thrust his hand and what it held thru her human chest and then into her Weelo body inside. Moon Dance gasped and human blood gushed from the huge puncture wound In Rio Rosa's body. Withdrawing his hand, Jack then waved his hand over the hole in Rosa's body and the gushing blood ceased and the wound healed itself instantly.

"What have you done?" Moon Dance screamed as all the painful emotions concerning Gray Feather's betrayal returned like a flood washing over her. Tears rolled down her face. It was almost more than she could bear and felt like the events of his sleeping with Pansy and Marrying Hissing Cat had just happened. In her mind she could see Gray Feather making love to Pansy on the Sand Dune. Also she saw Gray Feather fondling Hissing Cat after marrying her. Moon Dance doubled over in grief and gasped for air. She felt as though she were going to cease to be. She was experiencing too much emotional pain in one single moment. She could not breathe or speak for a moment.

Jack stood watching with big eyes. He had not expected that reaction. All he wanted was her to love her tribe enough to go beyond the web for them and become their new ruler with him.

"Why have you chosen to torture me in this fashion, Jack Benson?" She managed to spit out as she tried to calm herself and catch her breath.

"It was not my intention to torture you. I caught one of those shattered pieces of your heart when you threw them into the air for the hands of the web to have. I intended to use it one day to make you fall in love with me. However, I need you to have a heart to love your tribe again and help me do what is best for them. The piece of your shattered heart that I implanted in you will grow and become whole and full size again. Love your tribe again, Moon Dance. Love me. We need you!"

"I will not go with you, help you, or love you or them. You did not have the right to do what you just did. You have brought my worst nightmare back to life and I hate you for that. Yes, I may once more have a heart. However, I will use it to love my child and Dante with. They have not betrayed me. Get out of my sight Jack Benson and never return here. It was my choice to throw my shattered heart away. Now, I once more have hurts that I don't know how to deal with. You have caused me to love Gray Feather again, and that is the worst betrayal of all. Without a heart, I was free of him."

"Come with me now, Moon Dance. You may be hurting, but your tribe needs you. You are Weelo and always will be Weelo. That machete swinger is no one. Gray Feather is no one. They are both human. I am right for you. It is our destiny to lead our race." Jack Benson stated with an air of self-acclaim. "We are now royalty, Moon Dance!"

"Dante is who I have chosen and it will be Dante that I am faithful to. Leave and never come back here, Jack Benson. You have cursed me with a heart that loves again. In my thinking, that is not a good thing."

Moon Dance then ran in tears toward Dante who was waiting in front of the travel trailer for her with his machete drawn. She flew into his arms. In shock, Dante dropped his machete and wrapped his seventy plus year old arms around Rosa Moon Dance and held her tight. She had never shown any emotions before. He did not know what to think.

Moon Dance sunk into Dante's chest for comfort. The return of her heart had brought back the painful aching that went with Gray Feather's betrayal. She could not tell Dante that. Gray Feather was the skeleton in her closet that she could not talk about.

Jack Benson, seeing he was no longer welcome in Moon Dance's life, walked away in his new host body, a deceased Native American from the north named Little Elk.

Little Elk died in a car wreck on a deserted road late at night after a Saturday night of drinking. Only his wrecked car was found. Jack Benson, having just found entrance back into the Earth realm thru a dream catcher, caused Little Elk to crash. The dream catcher that Jack Benson traveled thru hung from Little Elk's rear view mirror. Jack Benson's sudden appearance in spirit form, in the seat next to him, was what caused him to wreck. He died. Jack Benson needed a host body. Little Elk had been a convenient one.

CHAPTER THIRTEEN

When The Night Winds Blew

Moon Dance spent a long miserable day trying to deal with her returning emotions. She could not tell Dante why she was in such a tearful state. So, she lied and told him that Jack Benson had brought her word that a friend from her past named Hissing Cat had died and that her tears were that of grief. He comforted her and made her tea with a shot of something in it that was not lemon. By the end of drinking the cup, Moon Dance was in a much lighter mood and prepared to see those arriving for evening readings beneath the Cottonwood tree down by the Rio. She was feeling so good, that she was sure that Dante had spiked her tea to help her quit crying. It had worked and she felt as light as a feather. He had also kept Carol Sue occupied while she spent the morning in tears and what he thought was grief.

"Rosa Moon Dance, you have a grandmother waiting for a reading. She is very old and I don't know how she got here. She says she once owned a ranch north of here. She looks very frightened and nervous, Rosa. I think she has walked many miles in her moccasins to make her way here. Also, she is wearing one of those hospital gowns that have the two little ties in back. She wears nothing else, Rosa."

"Tell her to walk on down to the Cottonwood tree and be seated. If she has walked away from a nursing home somewhere, we will take her to town in the pickup and see that she gets back to wherever it is that she has run away from. Nursing homes are not always pleasant places, Dante. I will be a minute. I need a moment or so to dry my tears and fix my face." She replied.

"Drink all of your hot tea before going, Rosa. It will help you get thru the evening and dull your grief. Drink it for me!" Dante stated grinning.

Moon Dance picked up her cup to please him and downed the brew. She never wanted to hurt him like she had been hurt. Now that she had a heart, she would make herself love him, she already respected him. Drinking all of his special tea was a matter of respect. She had also made up her mind that she was going to invite Dante to her bed. She wanted him, Carol Sue, and herself to be a real family. Also, the body she was in was capable of producing them a human child, a sibling for Carol Sue. Moon Dance was tired of being alone and she knew that Dante was too. There was no reason for them not to be there for each other in every sense. They were already devoted to each other as companions. She wanted to make love to a man again and have a man she trusted make love to her.

"You will feel okay by the time you reach the Cottonwood." Dante laughed and turned to exit the trailer.

"Dante, wait!" She called. He turned back around to see what she wanted.

"When the night winds blow tonight and Carol Sue is asleep, would you consider coming to my bed."

"What?" he asked in shock. Moon Dance was in her twenties in human years and he was over seventy.

"I am lonely, Dante. I want you to sleep with me and make me feel like a woman again. It has been a long time since I have been with a man, several years. If you are willing, I would like a child by you, a brother or sister for Carol Sue. I want you to take your rightful place in my bed. You have slept by the door long enough."

"It is my special tea talking in you, Rosa Moon Dance. We will discuss this tomorrow. When the night winds blow tonight, I will go hunting. Should I stay here, I might be tempted to take up the offer. You are a very beautiful woman. However, I would not want you to wake up tomorrow and use my machete to remove my manhood. When the night winds blow, I will go hunting. We need meat for our table. You do not need me in your bed. I am an old man and will not live long enough to raise a child to adulthood. I am sure I will probably leave you before Carol Sue is grown." Dante stated with a sudden faraway look in his eyes.

With that said, Dante turned and left the travel trailer. Then Moon Dance really cried. She couldn't even convince her Dante to make love to her. She hated her returned heart and the emotions it caused her to feel.

After a few minutes of tears, she left the trailer and headed for the Cottonwood tree to read for the evening. Carol Sue, as usual, was following Dante around as he piddled with this and that as he kept watch with his machete always at his side. He was her protector, but had turned her down as a lover. Moon Dance was sure that Jack Benson would have gotten a big laugh out of that, had he been a little bird listening in; especially when she had gone on and on about her and Dante being a couple. She felt a little humiliated.

As Moon Dance reached her reading table beneath the Cottonwood tree, she saw that it was Song Bird waiting for her and she was scantily dressed in a hospital gown. Moon Dance glanced down at her elderly friend's feet. They were dirty and bleeding from having walked thru the desert barefoot.

"Good Morning, Song Bird." She greeted her friend after seating herself in the chair across from the elderly woman. She ignored the way the elderly woman looked. She was older and deserved respect. She ignored the fact that Song Bird's white hair was loose, uncombed, and looked like the mangy tail of a dog. The Song Bird she remembered always had her long white hair perfectly braided and with a feather in it. This Song Bird looked like she might have slept outside for several days. She was not a pretty sight. "Have you come for a reading of the Tarot?"

"Cut the crap, Rosa. You know as well as I do that I was the one who taught you to read the cards after you stole a deck from the store in town. You were a border crosser and I taught you to read the Tarot so you could make yourself a living."

"Oh . . . ," Moon Dance replied not realizing that Song Bird and Rosa had a history. "I have played the Tarot Reader witch part too long."

"That you have." Song Bird shot back. "I need help and I don't know who else to ask. You owe me, Rosa."

"What do you need help with?" Moon Dance asked in reply.

"You always were a little dense, Rosa. You heard the hummers when I hid you in the top of my barn when you were a border crosser. You left the ranch because you said a strange light would appear on the third floor and a colored skin being would stand over your bed eyeing you. No one believed you back then. Even I, at first, thought you were dreaming. I believe you now. I saw a hummer the evening Night Hawk and the baby disappeared. She had blue skin and had a child with her, a little girl. They took Night Hawk and Millie's baby. You saw the light, heard the humming, and saw a being with purple skin before fleeing the ranch. I want you to tell me what you saw again. I am sorry I laughed back then. My disrespect of you drove a wedge between us. I am here to say I am sorry for not believing you and ask for your help. White Eagle is alone on the ranch. If you don't help me, the hummers may snatch him like they did his mother, Night Hawk, and the baby."

"I see . . . ," Moon Dance stated biting her lip and thinking about Rio Rosa who had her own closet and skeletons. "Why don't you ask Tall Willow to help you?" She asked knowing that he had disappeared, possibly gone home by light port without her.

"Tall Willow is one of them, Rosa. He opened the human body that he was living in. He wanted me to go to hell with him, some place he called Plutonia. He was a purple Kachina, a devil. I ran from him when I saw who he really was. I am a good Catholic. I know about possessions and how you must flee from the devil before he gets you. You saw a purple skinned man. I saw one and he was my Tall Willow. Now, I have seen a blue skinned demon woman."

Moon Dance wanted to laugh, but once more she bit her lip. It was amusing that humans thought aliens were demons. However, they did snatch dead human bodies to live in.

"Have you seen Tall Willow since then?" She asked, wanting to know what had happened to him.

"No, he and sleeping Moon walked out into the desert one night. When we found them, their bodies looked like they had been ripped open by animals. I think Tall Willow decided if he couldn't have me, he would seduce my grand-daughter, Sleeping Moon. A Kachina devil more powerful than both of them ripped them to shreds." She replied.

Again, Moon Dance bit her lip. Tall Willow was one of Plutonia's most re-nowned scientists. Song Bird had been privileged to be loved by one of the universe's elite, and was not aware of it. On Planet Plutonia, the elite did not marry beneath themselves. Song Bird was a far step down for him.

"Perhaps your purple skinned Kachina was actually in love with you." Moon Dance replied simply.

Song Bird grinned. "Tall Willow and I spent many nights butt naked in each other's arms. I will have to say, making love to that devil was pleasurable. I miss making butt naked love to him and him making butt naked love to me."

Moon Dance lost it and snorted. "I should be so lucky. I am having trouble se-ducing and keeping a butt naked lover. I am only in my twenties. I tried to seduce an older man for a lover just before you arrived. He turned me down. I think I might possibly need some tips from you."

Then Song Bird snorted. "You and I are alike, Rosa. We are strong women who choose who we want to be with. I am sorry that my grandson Night Hawk chose Millie to marry instead of you. She was way beneath his status in life, a damn bar fly. You are a self made strong woman. I don't know what he saw in her!"

"I do not wish to speak about Night Hawk, Song Bird. I don't know what I was thinking by seeing him. He was beneath me. A girl should never marry or go with anyone that has less than she does. I own these ten acres along the Rio. Your grandson owned nothing. The ranch was yours, as I recall." Moon Dance replied trying to say what she thought Rio Rosa would have wanted said. "I will say that I am sorry that your Night Hawk is missing.

"Will you drive me out into the desert in your pickup in the direction Night Hawk walked that night? White Eagle refused when I asked him. He put me in a nursing home for crazy old people instead. There has to be a clue out there as to what has happened to him. My daughter, many-many years ago also was walking in the same direction the night she disappeared. Tall Willow and Sleeping Moon's bodies were also found in that direction. Four people from one ranch do not disappear like that. I think there is a camp of Kachina hummers out there in the desert are snatching people. I need to know, Rosa. You and I are the only ones that have seen the purple and blue skinned beings, other than Charlie Elkhorn and he is denying what he saw the night the baby was taken. I also don't have anywhere to go Rosa. I need to stay with you. If I go to the ranch, White Eagle will just call for an ambulance and send me back. You once needed me many years ago. It is time for you to return the favor."

"You and I were always at odds when I dated Night Hawk. You didn't think I was good enough for him. Why should I help you? I was a far better choice than Millie?"

"It was your love of poker that I objected to, Rosa. I feared Night Hawk would marry you and one day you would gamble away what I left him. My husband and I started from nothing and worked hard for our wealth and big ranch. I would not even marry Tall Willow, in fear of his distant family laying claim once I was gone. I wanted the ranch to be passed down, not squandered on lovers and gamblers."

"Well, at least you are honest with me. That is more than most people have been."

"Will you help me and hide me from White Eagle? Your trailer is the last place he will look for me. I once hid you when border patrols were looking for you."

"I will help you, Song Bird. However, you must understand that I have a man up at the trailer named Dante that has become my companion. He has a little girl that lives with us. Her name is Carol Sue Dante. You must never tell them who you are, or question how they came to live with me. I rescued them from the river like I once did you." Moon Dance replied half lying. "I will tell Dante that you are a runner and have escaped a nursing home on the Mexico side. You can be our child's grandmother. No one will ever question it. I will tell everyone I have brought you from Texas to live out your years with me."

"Thank you, Rosa. I have no home to go to. I signed everything over to White Eagle just before he had me committed."

Moon Dance motioned for Dante with his machete to come down to the reading table beneath the cotton wood tree. He did as he was bid to do.

"Dante . . . meet Song Bird. She has escaped from a nursing home on the Mexico side. She is too old to travel further. We need a grandmother and babysitter for Carol Sue. She has come from Ft. Worth, Texas to live with us, if anyone asks. She is like you and has no green card. She will stay in the trailer when anyone questionable is around."

"I understand." Dante replied. "Do we clean her up before we keep her?" He asked laughing.

"I will clean you up, you tall piece of Hispanic, machete swinging, cactus crap." Song Bird replied standing.

"Perhaps I will let her stand guard over you with my machete. I think she could handle the job. Perhaps I should take on the role as the grandmother in our family." Dante returned fully amused with Song Bird who did not fear getting in his face.

"Take her to the trailer, Dante; find her a set of my clothes that are appropriate for her. Then was, comb, and braid her hair. She is older than us and we must treat her respectfully. She will be good for Carol Sue, someone new to play with. You will be free to hunt more and do other things around here."

"That is a good thing, Rosa Moon Dance. I will need to hunt more with another mouth to feed."

"She is very old, Dante, and won't eat much. If we are ever short on food, give her half of my plate."

"I will never short you or Carol Sue on food, Rosa Moon Dance. She will get half of mine, if it is needed."

Dante then escorted Song Bird slowly to the travel trailer. She was barefoot and her heels were bleeding; not to mention that her naked, sagging buttocks were shining out the back of the hospital gown she had on. Song Bird was weak from her days of walking and having not eaten. However, she had made it home to her new family. Her old life had stripped her naked.

~   ~   ~

Mid-afternoon, Dante approached Moon Dance after a client had left the reading table beneath the cottonwood tree on the bank of the Rio.

"What is it?" She asked him softly seeing that another client was waiting up by the travel trailer for her turn.

"Carol Sue is being occupied by her new grandmother. I need to hunt. There is a rabbit for our dinner, but nothing for breakfast. Will you be okay till I return?" he asked

"I will be fine, Dante. If you come across a wild boar, a little ham for breakfast would be a real treat. If you cannot find one, I can always catch a rattlesnake and grill him for breakfast tomorrow."

Dante rolled his eyes. He did not like Rattlesnake meat. "I will bring you a boar, even if I have to steal it from one of the rancher's pens. You know how much I despise rattlesnake."

Moon Dance laughed. "Ham it will be then."

Dante hugged Moon Dance's shoulders, kissed her on the top of her head, and then he slipped away into the desert. If Carol Sue saw him go, she would want to hunt with him. He had a secret, a mission to fulfill. It did not include a six year old tag-along. There was a gathering taking place in the desert and he was part of it.

CHAPTER FOURTEEN

The Headless Corpse

After reading for her next client, Moon Dance returned to the travel trailer and watched as Song Bird, taught Carol Sue how to braid hair. Having a little time for herself, she got lost in her thoughts about Gray Feather and her tribe that were possibly all dead, having been eaten by cannibals. With a returned heart, she had mixed emotions about possibly going to rescue Gray Feather, if he was alive. Her returned heart loved him. That was not a good thing. She had been a fool over him twice. Even knowing that, she had this over-whelming urge to make her way to planet Weelo and just peek at him at a distance.

As the sun dipped in the horizon and shadows fell across the desert, Moon Dance fried the single rabbit that was left in their meat supply. She then fed Carol Sue and Song Bird most of it. It was more important that they had the nourish-ment, than her-self. Song Bird hadn't eaten in a couple of days and Carol Sue was in a growing spurt. Both of them needed the food worse than she did.

After her two charges ate, Moon Dance cleaned up the kitchen and then joined Song Bird who was sitting on the stoop in front of the trailer enjoying the night breezes that were blowing.

"When will you go into the desert with me to search for Night Hawk and his child?" Song Bird asked.

"Now is as good of a time as any. Dante has gone hunting and Carol Sue has fallen asleep. She is a sound sleeper and will not wake up till she smells breakfast cooking in the morning. We will leave her here and lock her in." Moon Dance replied.

"The child will be okay?" The elderly Indian woman asked.

"Dante and I have told her, if she awakes and finds the door locked, it is because we have entered the desert to hunt for meat. She knows not to open the door till one of us returns. We have to hunt regularly to survive. We go to town as little as possible. Anyway, Carol Sue knows our routine. The worst that can happen to her is that she gets into the sugar jar and makes herself a sugar sandwich. She has a sweet tooth that is unbelievable."

"She is what the white man calls a latch key kid." Song Bird replied.

"Yes, I guess that is how they would see her. However, she is much too young to be one. We have made her one out of necessity."

"I am ready to search the desert if you are, Rosa. We can take the back road and then enter into the desert behind my former ranch house. Do you have flash-lights?"

"I have something better than that. The truck has a spotlight on it. Dante uses it sometimes to find deer or wild boars when we are desperate for meat. If there is anything on the desert within fifty feet of the truck, we will be able to see it." She replied wondering if she should let the grandmother discover the bones of Night Hawk's missing baby. She was sure that wild animals had eaten all of its flesh by now. Perhaps the discovery would still the restlessness and wondering in the old woman's soul.

"A spot light is a good thing, Rosa. Devils don't like light. Anyway, that is what my priest told me. Truthfully, I think he is full of book learning and has no experience in such matters. My parents followed the Great White Spirit. I am thinking of returning to the old ways and its religion. They at least believed in Kachina and knew how to deal with them. I threw holy water on the blue skinned being I saw. It did nothing to the demon woman. She looked at me like she was in shock, but the water did nothing. It had no magic."

Moon Dance bit her lip. She was the one that Song Bird had thrown the water on. "How far out into the desert do you wish to go before we start searching?"

"The ranch hands, when Night Hawk disappeared, scoured the desert floor for at least seven miles out. That was how the family of border crossers with slit throats was discovered. I fear the same has happened to my grandson and that a Kachina with a big knife is killing and abducting humans for some reason."

"It would have taken a very tall man to have overpowered Night Hawk." Moon Dance replied. "I doubt if just anyone could have done it. Is there a chance that the baby kid-mapping event just traumatized him and he has had a mental snap and just walked away like Millie did?"

"The border crossers didn't just walk away." Song Bird retorted with an annoyed voice. People had a habit of not believing her.

"Tell me about the border crossers and where they were found. We will start our search from there."

"There were five of them, a mama, papa, and three pre- teen boys. They were found about five miles out in the desert, just off the abandoned road behind the ranch that goes nowhere. A straw doll was found with them. Law enforcement thinks there was also a little girl. They do not have a clue as to what might have happened to her."

"Boys play with dolls when they are a little on the feminine side." Moon Dance threw out trying to get off of the subject of the missing little Hispanic girl. "Have you forgotten Mr. Mason's gay son? He stayed with you for awhile."

"I had forgotten that, Rosa." Song Bird snickered. "I caught him one night using my face crème."

Moon Dance snickered. "There are more Jerome Masons out there. One of the younger dead boys may have been a girl in a boy's body. The doll could have belonged to him."

"You may be right, Rosa."

Moon Dance took one last quiet peep at Carol Sue. She was dead to the world. Then, very quietly, Moon Dance and Song Bird exited the trailer and then locked the door. Then they got into the old, weather beaten, rusted out, green pickup and headed out to search for hummers, as Song Bird called them. Moon Dance was just appeasing the grandmother. Plus, it was a pleasant night to take a ride.

About five miles out into the desert, they came across a bunch of yellow tape that was whipping in the night breeze. It was caught on the spikes of a cactus. Moon Dance slowed the truck. She knew it had to mark the place where the family had been found.

"The family of border crossers was found here, Rosa." Song Bird stated pointing in the direction of the yellow law enforcement crime scene tape. "They all had their bodies slit open from their necks down to their crotches. My ranch hand, Pete, threw up when he found them. Their heads were missing."

Moon Dance slapped her hand over her mouth, realizing that there were aliens in the desert besides her-self. They could be Weelo, Plutonian, or from some planet she was not familiar with. Then she had another thought cross her mind. Dante had said the family that had tried to swim the Rio had been washed downstream and drowned. He had been gone way too long that night and then returned with a little girl. Could the family have died from his machete and he loaded them in the pickup and dumped them in the back desert? Did he do it for her, so they could have a child? Where were their heads?

Suddenly in shock at her suspicion, Moon Dance gagged and felt really ill. Immediately, she stopped the truck, opened her driver's door, and threw up. Then she leaned back in the truck seat for a moment to regain her composure.

"Are you pregnant, Rosa?" Song Bird asked innocently.

"I think the rabbit we ate must have upset my stomach. I am not pregnant, Song Bird. It is probably the wrong time of the year for us to be eating rabbits."

"You have a wimpy stomach. I have an iron one and can eat anything without getting sick. You should stick to eating chicken soup." Song Bird replied in an old lady, know it all, voice.

"I definitely do have a wimpy stomach at the moment."Moon Dance replied starting the truck again. She then drove further down the back road into the desert. "How much further do you wish to go?" She asked, trying not to show how much in shock she was. There was every possibility that her Dante was a sociopath, a killer. Was he the reason that people were disappearing? She was totally appalled and hoped it wasn't true. Then she scolded herself for thinking such a thing. Dante was over seventy. He couldn't overpower a family of five. Also, he was kind and gentle with her and Carol Sue. He being a murderer was impossible.

"We have only come five miles, Rosa. I wish to go at least twelve miles out. That is about as far as a man could walk at night with no flash light. Night Hawk had taken his boots off at the door, before heading for the bedroom to check on me and the baby. He was in his stocking feet when he climbed out the window of the bedroom to enter the desert and chase after the Kachina that had taken his child."

"I pray he has not suffered the same fate as the family back there." Moon Dance replied. She used the term pray loosely. She was Weelo and did not embrace the religions of the humans. However, she felt that Rosa would have said something like that.

"Whatever his fate, I just want to know what has happened to him. I must know so that I can go meet the Great White Spirit in peace, when it comes my time." Song Bird added. "If a man has killed him, I can deal with that. However, if he has been taken by hummers, he may still be alive. There is no one looking for him but me."

As they neared the spot where Moon Dance and Carol Sue had hidden the corpse of the baby, she slowed the truck and flashed the spot light. She would not point and say there it is. If the grandmother spotted it, she would be okay with that. Moon Dance was sure that nothing now existed but bones. The elements and wild animals would have reduced it to that. There would be no unzipped flesh for the grandmother to view.

To Moon Dance's surprise, she saw no bones where she had left the tiny deformed corpse. Wild animals had probably dragged the tiny skeleton off into the desert. Then she had another thought. If Dante wasn't a killer, there was the possibility that a family of aliens, needing a host body for a baby, might have taken night Hawk's baby. Beings from advanced civilizations were capable of repairing human bodies. She had done it herself, down thru the centuries as she had need of new host bodies to survive.

"I do not see anything, Rosa. Keep flashing the desert with your light as we drive further out. There has to be a clue out here somewhere." The grandmother demanded.

Moon Dance did as she was told and they drove several miles further on the deserted back road that wasn't used anymore. The interstate coming thru had ended travel on it. It did not take long till Moon Dance felt out of her comfort zone. She had driven into a part of the desert she had not visited before. Taking her time, she drove slowly so Song Bird could glance from side to side. Suddenly, they came upon a gulley and the road crossed over a huge drain pipe.

"Stop here, Moon Dance. I wish to walk down the bank and look inside the huge pipe. It would be a good place for someone to take shelter if they were in trouble from the elements or hide from hummers. I must look to see if any of the missing is in it. Night Haw, his baby, Millie, and my daughter from years ago are not the only ones missing. There are about ten women that have come up missing in the last year from the towns around here."

Moon Dance stopped the truck, leaving it running and the lights on. She handed Song Bird a flashlight and then the two women exited the truck cab and made their way down the slight sandy incline to where the drain pipe opened in a dry stream bed. The grandmother was the first to flash her light into the dark drain that spanned the underneath side of the road. In the wet season, it let flash flood water from the washes pass under the road.

Suddenly, the grandmother gasped and held her heart. "Flash your light there, Rosa. Am I seeing what I think I am seeing?"

Moon Dance flashed her light in the direction she indicated and then gasped herself. Tangled up in a huge dead cactus that had washed thru and got lodged in the drain was a skeleton with its clothing tattered and weathered.

"It is a woman, Song Bird. The skeleton has what is left of a short red skirt and a low cut blouse on." Moon Dance stated after walking a few steps into the pipe and flashing her light to see better. She is missing her head!"

"I must take a closer look, Rosa. Shine your light so I don't fall and break a hip as I come in. I must take a closer look and see if it is my missing daughter."

Moon Dance did as she was instructed and flashed her light toward the feet of the grandmother so she could walk into the drainpipe safely. Then, Song Bird entered the drain pipe that was large enough to walk straight up in.

After making her way slowly to where Moon Dance stood with her light, Song Bird flashed her light on the headless skeleton and eyed it and what was left of its clothing closely. The skeleton had been there for a while. Wild animals and insects had devoured all of its flesh.

"It is not my daughter." Song Bird replied sadly. "She always wore long, full, Navajo type skirts like me. That is a barfly skirt and blouse."

"Did Millie wear clothing like that?" Moon Dance asked trying to let the grandmother discover on her own that the body was probably that of Millie.

"My grand-daughter-in-law was a bar fly. I warned Night Hawk about going to those places. He paid dearly."

"Did Millie wear a belt, Song Bird? There is a scrap of a one still around her waist. It has what looks like sequins on it." Moon Dance asked flashing her light up and down the corpse.

"Sequins . . . ?" Song Bird asked who then took a closer look at the skeleton's middle where a belt hung on the skeleton as well as being snagged up in the cactus' needles. "It is Millie's. She always wore flashy bar stool clothes, jewelry, and accessories. She liked anything that was glitzy, including my grandson's wallet."

"Do you think that Millie might have actually been in love with your grandson? Even barflies fall in love." Moon Dance replied remembering the night that Millie had stabbed and killed Rosa over Night Hawk. Thanks to Millie, she got a host body. Now she had Carol Sue and Dante and was the happiest she had been in years.

"That barfly was after my money, Rosa. I fooled her. The day before she and Night Hawk were married, I signed papers with my attorney, putting the ranch and all of its holdings into White Eagle's name. Night Hawk was penniless on his wedding day, except for whatever he might have saved and put in his own personal account over the years. She married a pauper."

"How do you think she got washed up here in this drain pipe? If she was leaving Night Hawk, finding out he was penniless, why would she enter the back desert. She was a city girl and it would have made more sense for her to hitch a ride into town on the interstate. She had to know that this back road led nowhere."

"The hummers took her, possibly from the ranch house just like they took the baby." Song Bird instantly replied. "There was humming the night she disappeared. There was humming the night my daughter walked out into the desert and did not return. There was humming the night Tall Willow and Sleeping Moon entered the desert and had their bodies cut open."

Moon Dance bit her lip. She, in her former life body of Sleeping Moon, and Tall Willow had unzipped their bodies in the desert and abandoned them because they were leaving the ranch and needed new host bodies to continue their existences on Earth. She was Weelo and Tall Willow was Plutonian.

"Is it possible that Millie was on the interstate and somehow fell into a flooding wash and was swept downstream here?"Moon Dance asked seeing how the skeleton was all tangled up in the cactus and other desert debris inside the drain pipe.

"No, Rosa. The hummers killed her somewhere out here and then threw her into a back desert wash. She has ended up here due to flash flooding after her death. Maybe one of the hummers needed a new head." Song Bird stated seriously.

Moon Dance wanted to laugh at the comment, but she controlled herself. "Do you wish to return to your ranch and tell White Eagle about finding her? I cannot get mixed up in this, Song Bird. Millie and I were both dating Night Hawk. Law enforcement might think I am involved. I have a child and Dante to think about."

"No, we will leave her here. I do not wish to have a bar fly buried with my ancestors who were good and honest people. This is her grave. Let her sleep here till her God or the Great White Spirit chooses to come for her. She will probably be here for a very long time. I don't think she was on speaking terms with either of the divine ones."

Moon Dance bit her lip again. Song Bird was funny at times.

"It is your choice, Song Bird." Moon Dance replied simply.

"Dirt to dirt, and ashes to ashes . . . she is in her grave."Song Bird stated turning to walk out of the drain pipe.

Moon Dance was relieved. She feared that Millie's head had possibly been sliced off by her Dante. She then told herself that she was letting her imagination run away. She had never heard Dante speak of knowing Millie. He arrived on the U.S. side of the Rio Grande after Millie had stabbed Rosa and she had taken over her body and life. Then, she wondered if this back area of the desert was being used as a harvesting field by beings from some planet other than her own. Why would they want heads? Then she dismissed the idea telling her-self that she was imagining things.

"How much further out into the desert do you wish to go, grandmother?" Moon Dance asked the old woman as they climbed back into the pickup.

"Do you hear the humming, Rosa?" Song Bird asked listening in all directions."

We must be near the purple skinned hummers. I am not crazy. Do you hear it?"

"Yes, grandmother, I hear the funny sound."

"Drive another two miles out into the desert, Rosa. I want to see if the humming gets louder or softer. If it gets louder we are headed for the hummers. I know they have taken my family, as well as Millie's head. "

"Two more miles, and then we must turn around. I do not have a lot of gas in this truck's gas tank. We save enough to make it back to the Rio." Moon Dance replied. "Dante will have my head if he has to walk out into this desert with a gas can to bring this truck home."

"I just wish to know if the humming gets louder. Two more miles will satisfy my curiosity." The old woman replied.

"If the humming gets louder, Song Bird, we will return in a few days after I fill the gas tank. I am as curious as you are."

The two women headed further out into the desert on the road that went nowhere. Moon Dance continued to flash the spotlight and at the same time listen for the humming. She wondered if there was possibly a Plutonian light port other than the one that opened up on Song Bird's ranch?

As they rode on out into the desert, the humming did seem to be getting louder.

Suddenly, the sky lit up with multiple bolts of lightning. However, there weren't any clouds.

"Do you see that?" Song Bird asked pointing to a shaft of lightning that seemed frozen like an ice sickle. The bolt of lightning touches the sky and the ground and does not go away."

"I see it, Song Bird. It looks like a permanent moon beam shaft with storm lightning flashes all around it."

"We have found the hummers, Rosa. Stop the truck." She demanded.

"Stop the truck?" Moon Dance asked thinking they should continue driving towards the light. She estimated that the beam of light was probably another five miles in front of them. "Why?" She replied.

"I am an old woman and my bladder is not so good. I cannot confront hummers having a full bladder. I need to pee. It would be embarrassing to be confronted by Kachina and be so frightened that I would pee on my-self or a good looking one of them. Tall Willow was a good looking hummer. I am single. I wouldn't want them to think I was an old woman."

Moon Dance bit her lip again. Grandmother Song Bird was witty and humorous in her way of seeing things. "I think emptying our bladders might be a good thing. Dante's tea has done a number on me."

So, after stopping the truck, the two women took turns walking a little ways out into the desert to take care of business. Before they could both get back in the truck, the frozen moonbeam shaft of light started fading and the humming stopped.

"Damn it . . . I almost had them." Song Bird spit out as she watched the beam of light, in the distant sky, go out.

Another two miles of driving out into the desert produced no further sounds or signs of Kachina hummers or those who were missing. Moon Dance was relieved to turn the truck around and head back home. She would return without Song Bird when the humming started again and see if there was a light port in the desert, a Plutonian one. Then there was also the chance that it was a port for unfriendly aliens from some planet she was unfamiliar with. She didn't want to risk getting Song Bird killed or harvested by some unknown being.

Song Bird dozed on the way home as the night winds blew.

CHAPTER FIFTEEN

The Coyote Path

When morning came, Dante was not sleeping on his pallet. Moon Dance was concerned. He usually slipped in quietly, late at night, after hunting in the desert and didn't wake anyone. After making a trip into the desert the previous evening, Moon Dance feared he was hunting something with his machete that was not wild game. She tried to give him the benefit of a doubt, but the thought nagged at her. Now, he was returning late like he did the night he went to rescue the family from the Rio. Also, of concern to her was the fact he was supposed to return with meat for breakfast.

"Maybe he has been here, put meat in the fridge, and gone back outside to fish in the Rio." She muttered rubbing her eyes.

Moon Dance now slept on a pallet in the floor near that of Dante. Song Bird was old. Moon Dance had given her and Carol Sue the bed.

Moon Dance rose from her pallet on the floor and checked the cabinet sink and then their small refrigerator to see if there was fresh meat there. There was none. She was alarmed, but thought perhaps he had hunted longer than he anticipated and was running late getting home. She would have to start their day without him.

When Dante hadn't shown up by mid-morning, Moon Dance walked out into the desert behind the trailer to look for a rattler. She found a small one which she quickly caught, took home, dressed, and fried in strips like it was bacon. Then she split the meat between the grandmother and Carol Sue. There was not enough meat for three. She told Song Bird and Carol Sue that she was dieting. They seemed okay with her excuse. After they were thru eating, Moon Dance cleaned up the tiny kitchen of the travel trailer and then headed down to the bank of the Rio to sit beneath the cottonwood tree and think.

The skeleton of Millie with its head cut off bothered her. Dante always brought his wild game home without its head. She hoped her suspicions were unfounded. Was it possible that he had killed Millie with his Machete? Then she thought about Night Hawk who was missing. Rio Rosa had hard feelings toward both Night Hawk and Millie. Was Dante killing whoever he thought might be a threat to her? Then she dismissed the idea because Millie had disappeared before Dante swam across the Rio to the United States side.

After doing some serious thinking down by the Cottonwood tree, Moon Dance returned to the travel trailer. Carol Sue was braiding Song Bird's hair for the morning. Moon Dance opened the tiny freezer door once more. Once more she closed it knowing it was empty. She then sat down in front of the grandmother who braided her hair. When Carol Sue was thru with Running Bird's, Moon Dance would then braid the child's.

Everyone kept busy for the morning doing this and that.

Noon came and Dante still had not made it home. At that point, Moon Dance was really becoming worried. There was nothing to feed Carol Sue for lunch. She and the grandmother could wait, but a growing child could not. She had a couple slices of bread left. Out of desperation, she spread the bread with butter and then sprinkled sugar on it to make a sugar sandwich. It was all she had to give her. Carol Sue was thrilled with the sweet sandwich. She had an unbelievable sweet tooth.

Moon Dance always started reading the Tarot for customers at noon. She took her place down by the Rio underneath the Cottonwood tree to read. Song Bird agreed to greet clients and send them down one at a time to her. Rosa's business, reading the Tarot, was growing. Moon Dance read on the average of five or six hours a day. Also, word had spread that she made medicine bags for protection against Kachina. The Native Americans of the area had an obsession with the story about those who came up missing in the desert. The medicine bag business was good. Even though her stomach growled, Moon Dance got her afternoon of reading put in.

When the sun lowered itself in the evening sky and Dante had not returned, Moon Dance became really worried. After her last client had left, she approached Song Bird.

"Dante should have been home this morning before we all woke up. I fear something has happened to him. I want to drive the old road into the desert looking for him. He always walks it going into the desert to hunt. I don't want to frighten Carol Sue. Will you watch her till I return?" Moon Dance asked handing the grandmother two avocados that one of her clients had brought her. Eat these to keep you and Carol Sue from starving, till I return. I will catch a rattler on the way back, if I can't find Dante."

"I do not understand why you catch Rattlers, Rosa. You are Hispanic, not an

Indian. When did you learn to catch, fry, and eat them?" Song Bird asked. "My Sleeping Moon became suddenly obsessed with catching rattlesnakes. She brought a live one into our kitchen and I had to shoot its head off."

Moon Dance bit her lip. She had entered the body of Sleeping Moon after she died in the hospital. It was her that held the snake when the grandmother, in fright, shot its head off. It had not been a pleasant day in her former life in the host body of Sleeping Moon.

"Dante has taught me to catch rattlers for food." She replied lying. "I think he might be part Indian."

"I will watch your child, Rosa. You be careful. Don't forget, there are Hummers out there in the desert. They may have taken your Dante last night. If so, you will never see him again. Night Hawk, my daughter, and Night Hawk's baby are missing. You saw what they did to Millie."

"I will be careful. Feed Carol Sue her avocado, make her bathe, and then put her to bed. If she asks, tell her I have gone to meet Dante in the desert to help him bring meat home."

"When will you be home, Rosa? I want to know an exact time so that I will know whether the hummers have snatched you."

"I should be home by breakfast. If I am not, wait till suppertime. If I am not back then, take Carol Sue and go to White Eagle. The two of you rear my and Dante's child."

"Dante is too old to be fathering children, Rosa. Is there anything you would like to tell me before you go off chasing Kachina and looking for him?"

"I still love your grandson, Night Hawk, in spite of Millie. Is that what you want to hear me say?" Moon Dance replied trying to keep up her act of being Rio Rosa.

"Is Carol Sue Night Hawk's secret daughter, Rosa?" Song Bird asked with a wishing in her eyes.

"She is Dante's, grandmother, just as I have told you. He had a younger wife and they lived across the Rio on the Mexico side. She died giving birth to Carol Sue. Dante swam the river with Carol Sue on his back. I rescued them. Both almost drowned. Night Hawk married Millie. I was heartbroken and Dante was lost in grief from having lost his wife in child birth. We found each other. Dante is a godsend to me." She stated lying about the wife and childbirth part.

"I loved Night Hawk and White Eagle's grandfather. He died and I met Tall Willow on a visit to the Mason's ranch. He was a god-send to me. Loving my grandson's grandfather was easy. He was gentle like White Eagle. However, loving a god-send man is even easier. You have passion for them. I have loved two men, one a Native American human and one a Kachina. I think I loved and wanted the Kachina named Tall Willow the most. Perhaps he put a spell on me. It was a very good god-send spell. I wish now that I had a love child by him. However, now that I know he is a Kachina, our love child would have been a little devil."

Moon Dance snickered. "I understand. I loved Night Hawk, but Dante put that special spell on me. He is my heart. I would have a love child by him, if he would agree. It is him that tells me no. He says he is too old to raise a child to adulthood."

"It is good that you have loved again, Rosa. Night Hawk was a womanizer. You deserve better. Millie was what he deserved. She took the wind out of his womanizing sails."

"Thank you, Song Bird. That means a lot to me."You are my god-send friend."

~   ~   ~

As the evening sun was started to drop in the western sky, Moon Dance drove Rosa's old green pickup once more into the desert and down the abandoned back road. She reached the spot where the family of five had been killed and their heads cut off. The sun was starting to fall behind a red rock range. There had been no sign of Dante, so she kept driving. Pretty soon, she came upon an Indian boy who appeared to be hunting for rabbits ten or so feet off the road. She slowed down, stopped and yelled at him asking him if he had seen a very tall Hispanic man, a hunter. The boy walked to the door of the truck and held up two rabbits he had shot. Moon Dance eyed a woman's necklace that was around his neck. It had a familiar logo on it.

"Those are two fine rabbits that are perfect for frying. " Moon Dance stated smiling at the boy. "That is a very interesting necklace you have on. Did you trade rabbits for it?"She inquired recognizing Song Bird's ranch symbol on it.

"I found it in the desert back there. A lady hunter must have lost it. It was very dirty when I found it, like it had been there for many years. I cleaned it up by spitting on it and rubbing it. It is a very nice necklace."

"What do you plan to do with the necklace?"

"I will bribe my mother with it. I will offer to trade the necklace to her in exchange for getting to stay up late for a whole week and not doing my homework."

As she talked with the boy, Moon Dance wondered if the lost necklace could have belonged to Song Bird's daughter, Night Hawk and White Eagle's mother, who had been missing for years.

"I like your necklace. Would you consider trading it to me for this fine bracelet I have on that is made from real silver and turquoise. It is embedded with these shining stones that are said to emit moonbeams?" She asked extending her arm with the bracelet on it for him to inspect. Rosa's jewelry box was full of shiny baubles that shined. Moon Dance wore what interested her from the jewelry box. She had to keep up her projected Rosa persona. The boy studied the bracelet.

"If I wanted your bracelet, you would ask two items in exchange. That is a good barter. You want my necklace. I think it would be a fair trade if you offered me two things in exchange for my fine spit polished necklace." The boy replied grinning. "My mama is very heavy. That bracelet would not go around her 'fat as a pig' wrist. It would not buy me any nights of staying up late. She would tell me to throw the bracelet in my toy box and give it to a girl someday."

Moon Dance glanced to see what was in the truck. On the dash was a new spool of fishing line that belonged to Dante. Also, there was a bag of peppermints. Chocolate melted in the desert. The candy of choice for carrying with you, or leaving in your vehicle for a mid day treat was hard candy. Dante had a thing for peppermints. Even they sometimes became sticky in their wrappers. This bag was a new one and the candy looked inviting.

"I will trade you my bracelet and this new spool of fishing line. You could catch many fish on it out of the Rio and trade them to your mother for staying up late."

"I am a hunter. Fishing is for old men with broken legs who cannot hunt. I have no need for the fishing line. I do not have a broken leg and I am not an old man." The boy replied still grinning which was a sign he was still bartering.

"What about my bracelet and this new bag of peppermints. It is a long way to town and these candies would taste great late tonight when you are sneaking out your window to stay up late. I know you sneak off into the desert with your dog and howl at the moon to keep from going to sleep. I bet your dog has very bad breath when he howls with you. One of these mints could make his howling breath much nicer to be in the presence of."

The boy quit grinning and asked, "How do you know my dog has bad breath?"

"I am Rio Rosa, the witch Tarot reader who lives in the trailer down on the bank of the Rio."

"The Great White Spirit has told on me, hasn't he? My mother comes to you for readings. She asks for guidance in raising me. I am a handful, or so she tells everyone. I bet she has asked you to inquire of the Great White Spirit for a cure for my dog's breath. Am I right? She says I smell just like my dog and I have his breath."

"It would please the Great White Spirit if you traded me that necklace for my bracelet and this bag of mints." Moon Dance replied trying not to laugh. "He told me so!"

"The Great White Spirit and I haven't been too friendly lately. I got crap for my birthday. I asked him for a four wheeler." The boy replied once more grinning. Then he whispered before Moon Dance could respond. "I have decided to dump him as my god and convert to being a Baptist. Kids in the Baptist church get candy, soft drinks, coloring pages, and other goodies every Sunday. The Great White Spirit doesn't give me crap on Sundays."

"Perhaps you should believe in your Great White Spirit, but attend the Baptist's Sunday school and reap your share of the goodies. A smart boy would take advantage of freebies."

"That makes sense. Maybe I will attend the Methodist church one Sunday a month when they have their church dinner. I like chocolate cake and they always serve it."

"You are a smart boy. You should also attend the Presbyterians once in a while. At Christmas time, they give great big charity baskets of food that always have candy and toys for children in them."

"I think I will also embrace the religion of the basket church." He replied grinning and eyeing the bag of peppermints that Moon Dance was now holding out the window to tantalize him.

"Do we have a deal, your necklace for my bracelet and mints?" Moon Dance asked shaking the bag of peppermints.

"I still do not have anything to trade my mother for nights of staying up late." He replied folding his hands across his chest in Indian fashion.

"I will throw in a free reading of the Tarot cards. Your mother pays me twenty dollars for each of her readings. Trade your mama your free Tarot reading for a week of getting to stay up late." Moon Dance replied shaking the bag of breath mints once more.

"For my fine necklace, you will give me a free reading, a bag of mints, and your bracelet?" He asked not grinning which meant he was thru bartering. "I think I will keep it."

Moon Dance knew she was going to have to sweeten the deal.

"For your old necklace I will trade you my shiny new bracelet, a Tarot reading, a bag of mints, and throw in the spool of fishing line. That is my final offer." She replied also ceasing to smile to let him know she was thru bartering.

"Fishing line stored is a good thing. I don't need it now, but I could throw it in my toy box till I am old enough to have a broken leg. I can see myself someday being chased and tripped by my fifth wife. I am sure I will have a broken leg from trying to escape her broom." He replied."It is the fifth skinny wife that gets a warrior in trouble. Fifth wives are not fat and they can run fast and swing brooms hard."

Moon Dance lost it and laughed till there were tears in her eyes. When she was done, she asked thru her teary eyes, "You plan on having five wives?"

"The first four will get fat like my mama because I am a good hunter and will feed them well and take them to church dinners where there is chocolate cake. One will go with me to the Baptist dinners, the second the Presbyterian, the third the Methodist, and the fourth up to Pow-wow gatherings. I will need the fifth one, the skinny one to wear your skinny bracelet." He replied taking off the necklace from around his neck and holding it out.

Moon Dance immediately removed the bracelet from her arm and handed it along with the fishing line and mints to him. She then took the necklace, which she wanted to show to Song Bird, and hung it from her own neck for safe keeping. It had the grandmother's ranch logo on a medallion hanging from it. She felt sure that it possibly belonged to the grandmother's missing daughter. If it did, the boy could lead them to where he found it and possibly the bones of Song Bird's missing female, grown child.

After the exchange was completed, Moon Dance returned to her original inquiry.

"I am looking for a very tall, Hispanic hunter man named Dante who might be carrying a wild boar. Also, he would be toting a machete. Have you seen him while you have been on your hunt?"

"I saw a tall man with a machete about three hours ago in the back desert. He was hunting with a group of strange looking men. One was a dirty dressed Indian man and the others were naked. The naked men were chasing your hunter and the Indian down the tail of Turtle Wash." The boy replied as he picked up his two rabbits to leave.

"Why didn't they chase you?" Moon Dance asked trying to gather further information as to what Dante was up to.

"I hid behind a huge cactus. I did not approach them and they did not see me. I was not in the mood for a foot race." The ten or eleven year old boy replied. I just crouched and let them pass."

"That was very smart of you." Moon Dance replied suddenly in a panic. Why would anyone be chasing Dante and an Indian? She had never heard Dante speak of having an Indian hunting buddy. It just didn't make sense, other than Dante was now missing. "Would you be willing to show me where you saw the men running? I am not familiar with the back desert."

"What do you have to give me for my time? I am on my way home. If I get home late, my mama will beat my backside with her fat hands. I will show you, if you make it worth my while." He replied preparing to walk away in the direction of his home.

Moon Dance looked about in the cab of the pickup truck again. There was nothing there but the flashlight and she needed it. She ran her fingers thru a loose wisp of hair pushing it back from her face. Rosa wore her long hair in a long braid down the back. That was when she felt Rosa's dangling, feather and bead ear rings she was wearing. These are all I have left to barter with. You could give them to your mama and she might be so happy that she would forget about beating your backside and possibly let you stay up late tonight."

"You do not have anything else to offer?" He asked a little disappointed.

"No, that is all I have." Moon Dance replied.

"All right . . . However, I will not give those to my mama. I will take the back-side beating. The fine feather earrings I will save as a gift for whichever of my five wives is my favorite, someday when I am old."

Moon Dance grinned, bit her lip, and removed the earrings and handed them to him. "Just show me where you saw them three hours ago. Afterward, I will drive you back here to this spot. Then I will return to the back desert to look for my hunter, Dante."

"My mama has warned me not to speak with strangers or get in cars with them." He replied turning the ear rings over in the palm of his hand.

"I am a stranger; but also, I am not one. Your mother comes to me for Tarot readings." Moon Dance replied hoping he would show her.

"I will tell you where I saw them. You drive five or so miles further into the desert, park, and then hike down the three cactus coyote path till it reaches the clearing by Turtle Wash. The men I saw were running down the tail of the turtle when I last saw them. "As he held out the ear rings to give them back.

"I am not familiar with your coyote path or where along the back desert road to look for it. Please show me. You don't have to ride up here in the cab with me. You can ride in the back. That would not be getting in the car with a stranger."

"I will take my hunting knife to you, if you try anything." He replied pulling a pocket knife from his pocket and displaying it after laying the rabbits on to the desert sand."I thought I might have to use it on that group of purple skinned men, had they discovered me. However, I am good at stalking and hiding. They ran within ten feet of me and never saw me."

"Purple skin . . . ?" Moon Dance asked in shock. "Did you say purple skin?"

The Indian boy got the most sheepish grin on his face and he kicked a pebble on the sand before answering.

"I drank what was left in my father's beer can before I left our Hogan this morning. He was drunk and passed out in his chair. I was thirsty and needed a cold drink before hunting. It tasted really bad, but I drank the half of a can anyway. I think I was a little drunk when I saw your tall Hispanic man and his Indian friend playing chase with the five purple skinned men. My father sees things when he is drunk on wine. Once he saw a three headed raccoon riding on the back of a deer that had my mother's head on it." The boy replied grinning. "He shouldn't drink wine and I shouldn't drink beer. Beer causes me to see men with funny colored skin."

"I do not like the taste of beer either." Moon Dance replied returning the boy's sheepish grin. "Will you climb in the back of my pickup and show me where the coyote path is. The Hispanic man, that I am looking for, is very old. He may be hurt or have a broken leg. I am his fifth wife, the one who wears his skinny arm bracelet." Moon dance lied to keep the boy's interest.

"I will ride in the back of your pickup and show you where the path is. You drive slow and stop when I yell to do so. You try anything crazy with me, when we stop, and I will take my knife to you. Do you understand?" He replied picking up his rabbits.

"I understand. I will drive slowly and you yell 'stop' when you spot the coyote path."

"You will need to drive at least five miles further down this road into the back desert. I hitched a ride earlier with a hunter bringing me back out. He had red skin like mine, not purple. Indians you can trust. It is the white men and the Mexicans that you have to watch out for. Anyway, that is what my mama tells me. My papa is always too drunk to tell me anything."

"When your mother comes for her next Tarot reading, I will make sure I give her a reading that will cause your papa to sober up and pay attention to you. I will have a Kachina call on him." She replied thinking she just might confront the man and show him her blue self to scare him. She would tell him if he didn't sober up and spend time with the little boy she would return and take the little hunter into the land of the missing." White men and Indians were demon crazy. Charlie Elkhorn had run from her when he saw her in her blue skin. Song Bird had fainted. She was sure she could frighten one Indian man, who drank too much, into sobriety.

After the boy climbed into the back of Rosa's old green pickup with his rabbits and items he bartered for, Moon Dance drove further into the desert with the Indian boy in the back holding to the side of the pickup bed looking for his coyote path. About seven miles further into the desert, he yelled stop.

To Moon Dance's surprise, they were about a mile from where she and Song Bird had seen the frozen moonbeam of lightning in the night sky. When she parked along the shoulder of the road, the boy jumped out of the truck and pointed to a coyote path rambling off into the desert beside three huge cacti. She looked in the direction he was pointing. The path would be visible to a flashlight. Pulling a red sash belt from her waist, she tied it onto one of the three cacti. That way she could easily find the path again after taking him back and then returning.

"I saw the Hispanic man you speak of about a quarter of a mile down that path. The coyote trail leads to a clearing and a dry wash we Indians call Turtle Wash. It has four skinny washes or legs that empty into it. The main wash, which is wide, makes the turtle's head and the tail. There is a small spring in the head of the turtle. A pool of water stands there. The tail is dry and if you follow it, it will lead back to this road many miles behind us. This coyote path is the short way in and out to the turtle's head, the spring."

"If I follow this path, I will come to a clearing or dry wash where you saw the purple skinned men playing chase with my machete man and an Indian?"

"Yes. You will need to hike about a quarter of a mile into the desert, down this path. You will then come to the body of Turtle Wash. If it is dark and you can't find the coyote path to return to the road, follow the turtle's tail and the dry stream bed will eventually take you to the culvert bridge we drove over a few miles back that has a huge drain pipe beneath it." The boy stated pointing in the distance and which way the wash ran. The turtle's tail is winding and long. The purple skinned men and your Hispanic man and the Indian were running down the tail of the turtle when I saw them."

"If I get lost or cannot find the coyote path, due to darkness, I am to follow the tail of Turtle Wash. It will take me back to the low water bridge that has the huge drain pipe under it." She repeated mulling over his words.

"That is right." The boy replied.

Moon Dance knew that Millie's skeleton was in that drain pipe. Did Dante, the purple skinned men, the Indian, and Millie have some connection? Were the purple skinned men actually Plutonians and the frozen beam of lightning a light port?

"How purple was the five naked men's skin?" She asked as a final question.

"They were Lavender, like wild flowers." He stated laughing. "I hope you haven't drunk anything, if you intend to take the coyote path. If you have, you just might see my naked, purple Kachina men. My father sees a deer with my mother's head on it when he drinks."

"I have had nothing but water today." Moon Dance replied and then added after shaking her finger at him."Get back in and I will drive you back to the place where I picked you up. Afterward, I will return and look for my friend. He may still be hunting with your Lavender flower, Kachina."

The boy climbed in the truck bed of Rosa's old, green, pickup. It took about twenty minutes for her to return him to where she had first spoken with him. She then drove back to the coyote path where she parked and turned the head lights off. The sun had dipped below the horizon and night shadows were falling. She reached under the seat and pulled out the truck's flash light. Then she checked to make sure the batteries were good. They were, when she switched the light on and then off. She could walk a short ways into the desert before daylight was totally gone without needing to use it.

Moon Dance got out of the truck, removed her belt sash from the cactus, and then proceeded to follow the coyote path. She quietly followed the trail flashing her light when needed and keeping an eye out for Rattlesnakes. If she didn't find Dante, she would need a couple of rattlers to feed those living beneath her roof. She had become dependent up on Dante for meat. However, she feared his helping her may have come to a sudden end. If it had, she would have to become the hunter and provider for her new family.

Moon Dance worried about Carol Sue as she walked. She would have no way of explaining Dante's disappearance to Carol Sue. She had come to think of him as her father. It would be a serious blow to her emotional state to lose him. She was still having nightmares about being caged, stunned, and hung by her feet in the Planet Weelo slaughter house. Dante seemed to be the only one that could calm her and give her a sense of safety and stability.

As she was about half way to where she thought she should be on the path, she suddenly heard a faint humming. It was the same sound she and the grandmother had heard the night they discovered Millie's body in the drain pipe. She looked about in the desert to see if there was a shaft of frozen lightning. She didn't see one, but she was sure that she was near the spot where she guessed the moonbeam, frozen, shaft of lightning to be that night.

As she walked and listened, she felt the cool night breezes start to blow in from the Rio. She had hoped to find Dante before the cold night winds blew. She hadn't brought much to wear in the form of protection from the elements. She hadn't expected to be out after dark. Bartering with the Indian boy and returning him to where she found him had taken up at least an hour of what remained of daylight.

Now she was searching for Dante in the dark. She knew after midnight, the temperature would drop. However, she was not going to let that stop her from looking for him. It was hard for her to admit, but he had become her heart. Unlike gray Feather, Tall Willow, and Jack Benson, Dante had been there for her, till now. She knew he would never abandon her on purpose. Something had to be wrong.

Too Moon Dance's dismay, she found no clues as to Dante's whereabouts along the coyote path or in the wash, the body of the turtle. She walked a mile down the turtle tail, but found no evidence of five purple skinned men, an Indian, or Dante. Returning to the wash or body of the turtle, she realized that the faint humming had stopped. Disappointed, she returned to the road by the Coyote path, got in her truck, and returned home.

The necklace was the only thing she had found. She would show it to Song Bird when she woke up in the morning. She was sure that the grandmother and Carol Sue were in bed asleep. She guessed that it was somewhere around midnight.

CHAPTER SIXTEEN

Song Bird's Visitation

There is a niche in society for every man. Some are just late in life finding out what their purpose and life mission is. Song Bird, grandmother of Night Hawk and White Eagle, was in her eighties when she walked away and started over. Old doors have to close before new ones open. Song Bird was taking her place in the land of Indian medicine women, gypsies, witches, Tarot readers, and mediums. She did not realize that she could hear and see things others could not. Her seeing and hearing hummers had gotten her branded as crazy. Rosa Moon Dance was the only human she could turn to that shared her beliefs in the mystical and the possibility of aliens on Earth.

After Song Bird's grandson, White Eagle, placed her in a mental institution, she heard the call of the winds and they told her to return to the Rio Grande and to Rosa. She had climbed out a second floor window, climbed down a drain pipe, walked for three days barefoot, and made her way to her new home with Rosa and Carol Sue. It is in the starting over that man sometimes finds his true self.

It was late and the night winds were blowing. Song Bird lay in bed next to Carol Sue listening to the music of the blowing. It was a pleasant moment and she was thankful to have a new family to love and a roof over her head. She had spent over eighty years with her other family. They had stripped her naked and then caged her like she was a rabid dog. Now, she would spend her remaining years with a woman she had tried to keep her grandson, Night Hawk, from marrying. It had been a big mistake on her part.

Song Bird was embracing a lot of new changes in her life. Having a child to love named, Carols Sue, was a blessing, someone to hand her stories down to about the hummers. She had converted to Catholicism when she was young. She and her husband had been converted when they were first married. A Catholic mission had been built nearby. Now, she had decided to abandon the Catholic faith. The

Catholic god, she had been brainwashed into believing in, had not come to her rescue when she was locked up in the mental institution by her grandson. She had prayed, but the white man's god did not come. When no answer came, she had to save herself. Now, she would return to the Great White Spirit and embrace the old ways and who she was, a Native American who believed in Kachina and sky walkers.

Listening to the night winds blow, Song Bird slipped into an in-between state, the place you enter before going fully asleep or just before waking. Her long white hair, which had never been cut, was braided and draped over one shoulder of her reclined body. The very long Indian braid lay with one coil in it and the end, with a feather attached, trailing off the side of the bed as she dozed. The feather on the end of the braid was fluttering and moving as if some mystical night force was causing it to do so.

As she lay there half asleep and half awake, Song Bird thought she heard a male voice calling her. In her dream like state, she strained her ears to listen and determine what the voice was trying to tell her. Then she realized that it was the voice of the Great White Spirit.

"What do you want, Great White Spirit, god of my ancestors?" She asked in her in-between worlds trance state.

"A medicine woman who reads at the table beneath the Cottonwood tree . . ." The voice of thunder drums replied.

"Who is the medicine woman you wish to read beneath the Cottonwood tree?" She asked in reply.

"You are the one." The Voice of the Great White Spirit replied.

Then there was silence and Song bird drifted further into the state of sleep. The feather at the end of her braid quit fluttering.

~   ~   ~

Moon Dance returned home, slipped in the travel trailer, and fell into restless sleep on her pallet on the floor. Dante was still missing; his sleeping rug was not spread out. Moon Dance checked his sleeping spot just about every hour during the night. She was sure he had to be dead, possibly killed by the purple skinned beings that the Indian boy had seen. She was torn and worried sick. For the first time, she realized that she had fallen in love with Dante, in spite of the fact that her heart still ached for Gray Feather. She wanted her love for Gray Feather to go away, letting her be happy with her feelings for Dante. Dante had been good to her and she was sure he would never betray her. She wanted the security of his love and arms. She just had to convince him to accept her love. He had turned her bed down before he came up missing. She did not see their age difference as a problem, but he seemed to. Dante was over seventy years old and her host body was in her twenties. Dante did not know she was an ancient soul that had been stepping down thru the centuries from one host body to the next. She was afraid to tell him. Charlie Elkhorn had called her a demon when she showed him her blue Weelo body.

Morning came finally. Dante still had not returned. When the morning sun peeped in the windows of the travel trailer, Moon Dance made her way to the bedroom to check on Song Bird and Carol Sue. The little girl was sitting up in bed listening to the grandmother snore and seemed amused with it. She was tickling the grandmother's nose with a hawk's feather that had worked its way out of the grandmother's braid. Moon Dance grinned and then picked her up from the bed and carried her in her pajamas into the kitchen of the tiny travel trailer and then stood her down on the floor to dress her.

Moon Dance had not snored or slept peacefully. She knew that she had to return to the desert to hunt for Dante. This time, she would take Carol Sue with her and let the grandmother sleep. She also decided to take Carol Sue's dog named Fish Tail along. He hated strangers and barked fiercely when they approached. During the hours she did readings, Fish Tail was kept locked in the travel trailer. He was a no-breed mutt who had a tail that had been broken at some point. His tail pointed up and then suddenly straight down. He had swum the Rio one day to Carol Sue after she whistled for him. He never returned to the Mexico side. He seemed content to be Carol Sue's companion. It was strangers he hated, especially white ones. If Dante was lying hurt in the desert, Moon Dance felt that the dog would find him. Carol Sue's dog was just as crazy about Dante, who kept him well fed on wild game.

"Why does grandmother Running Bird sleep so sound and make such funny noises with her breathing?" Carol Sue asked as Moon Dance dressed her.

"She is in the land of dreams. She sleeps deep. Come! We are going to go into the desert to look for Dante. He went hunting again this morning. I think he might possibly need us to help carry his game home. We will let the grandmother sleep in. She will need to watch you later in the day when I have clients to read the Tarot for." Moon Dance replied, not wanting to upset Carol Sue with the possibility that Dante was gone forever.

"Dante always watches me. My new grandmother is too old to chase frogs on the banks of the Rio and rabbits in the desert. She probably squirms if asked to put a worm on a fishing hook."

"That is so, she is old and squirmy." Moon Dance replied softly as she finished dressing Carol Sue and grabbed for the truck keys which were on a hook by the door. "However, the grandmother chased a lot of frogs and rabbits when she was your age and they were probably bigger and faster hoppers. I bet she has great stories that she can sit and tell you as you chase the frogs on the banks of the Rio."

"I like stories. Do you suppose she has any girl stories? Dante tells me all boy stories." Carol Sue asked in a serious voice. "He tells me lots of stories about three little boys who live on a far away planet who are studying to be scientists. I am tired of little star boy scientist stories."

"I am sure Grandmother Song Bird has a lot of girl stories including one about an old girl who shot the head off of a rattlesnake and she was half blind." Moon Dance added as she walked to the truck with Carol Sue, opened its door, and helped her in. She then whistled for Carol Sue's dog and let down the tail gate for him to jump in. Then she closed it and got in the driver's side of the pickup. She felt she did not have a choice. She had to go look for Dante. He had become her heart.

~   ~   ~

Moon Dance feared she had missed seeing Dante the night before, due to it being dark. If he was hurt, ill, or dead; she could not leave him in the desert. It didn't take but about twenty minutes and she arrived in the back desert at the Coyote path. After parking Rio Rosa's beat-up pickup, she led the way down the coyote path, heading for Turtle Wash. There was nothing on either side of the path that suggested that anything was not as it was suppose to be. Jack Rabbits hopped away from them and lizards scrambled for hiding places. Birds sang and the morning air was chilly in spite of the sun giving off a pleasant warm glow.

Moon Dance had put an extra long sleeve shirt on Carol Sue to protect her from the early morning chill. However, she had failed to do so for herself. She rubbed her arms which were covered with goose bumps. It was six six-thirty in the morning. She scolded herself for not bringing a long sleeve shirt for her-self.

Reaching the body of Turtle Wash, Moon Dance stopped for a moment and looked about. She had not checked out the body of Turtle Wash, the previous night, due to the Indian boy telling her that he saw Dante and the others running down the tail of the turtle toward the drain pipe low water bridge. She had not found any sign of Dante or the others in the tail of the turtle. This morning she would search the dry bed of the wash, or the body of the turtle. She also hadn't checked the head of the turtle where the boy said there was a small spring and pool of water.

It did not take her and Carol Sue long to reach the body of Turtle wash. She then made the decision to walk the rim or bank where she could look down into the dip in the Earth and see anything that might be out of normal there. Also, she wanted to check around the house size boulders that loomed at the far end of the turtle's body, by the neck.

"Why are we walking the edge of this dried up creek bed?" Carol Sue asked as she trailed along behind Moon Dance. Before listening for a reply, Carol Sue whistled for her dog which had taken off in a running frenzy chasing a road runner that there was no way he was going to catch.

"We are looking for Dante. He may need our help carrying meat home. He hunts here."

"Oh yea. . . "She replied in her childish little girl voice. "I forgot. Will we find him soon? My feet are tired and I haven't had my breakfast yet."

"I want to check behind those huge boulders up ahead. If Dante isn't there, we will return to the truck and go home. How would you feel about fried rabbit for breakfast? I think Fish Tail could catch one of those long eared Jack Rabbits, if you told him to."

"Get a rabbit!" Carol Sue yelled at her dog with glee.

Moon Dance needed the distraction for Carol Sue till she checked out the boulders.

Reaching the far end of the dip in the earth, Moon Dance circled the three huge boulders looking between them for any sign of Dante or him having been there. The leaning rocks would have made a good shelter for someone who was lost or hurt. As she rounded one, she stopped in her tacks. A few feet ahead of her lay a bloody corpse on the ground, and its head was missing. The headless body looked familiar. After looking about, she made her way to the dead body and carefully turned in over from its stomach. She gasped when the corpse turned from lying on its stomach to flopping down on its back. She recognized the turquoise belt buckle as belonging to the Indian body that Jack Benson had been using for a host. She slapped her hand over her mouth in fright, to keep from yelling and alerting Dante or one of the purple skinned men that might still be in the area. Had Dante beheaded Jack Benson's host body with his machete?

After quickly calming herself, she stood to return to Carol Sue and get out of the back desert as fast as possible. Danger lurked and she wasn't sure just exactly what the danger was. Millie had been beheaded. Whoever was killing people in the desert would not think twice about killing her and Carol Sue. That person, as bad as she hated to consider it, could be her own Dante.

Moon Dance didn't concern herself with the host body of Jack Benson. He was a Weelo being like herself. His host body might have been killed violently, but he would have exited it in his spirit form and just flew off to find another host body. It was the killer that she feared. She had grown comfortable in her new life as Rio Rosa and did not want to have to go looking for another host body. Also, children's host bodies were hard to find. If the murderer attacked and killed the host body Carol Sue was in, Moon Dance was not sure she could find one. Without a host body, Carol Sue would cease to be in 24 hours.

Then, as frightened as she was, Moon Dance had a moment of amusement and muttered, "Well, Jack, when the killer cut off the head of this host body, I hope he didn't cut off the head of your Weelo body too. I can just see you out there somewhere carrying your head like the fabled headless horseman."

Having Carol Sue's safety to think about, Moon Dance then hiked hurriedly in the direction of the desert where the dog was barking and chasing a rabbit. She needed to quiet the dog and back track quickly.

As she was retreating, she noticed an abandoned, long sleeve, flannel shirt lying on the sand by one of the boulders. Still cool and having goose bumps from the early morning chill, she picked it up, After looking it over for spiders and scorpions, she gave it a good shaking and then put it on. The man was tall and thin that had worn it. Fading said it had been in the desert for awhile.

Moon Dance was disappointed that she had found no sign of Dante anywhere. However, she was glad to have stumbled upon Jack Benson's head free host body. She knew he was alive and well, but looking for a new host body somewhere to enter. As she hurriedly walked toward the sound of the barking dog, she told herself she would return in a few days and check out the spring and pool that made up the head of the turtle. Now was not a good time; knowing that Jack Benson's host body was a fresh kill.

Moon Dance quickly found Carol Sue, picked her up, and carried her exiting the desert. She was too big to carry at age six, but Moon Dance didn't want her trailing behind, whistling, or attracting a possible killer's attention. There was no guarantee that the killer was not still in the desert and looking for a new victim. She hoped the murderer was not her Dante. He often threatened to cut off people's heads with his machete when threatened. Maybe he had not returned home because he was on a killing frenzy. She had heard about human sociopaths.

As she walked, she knew that she could never bring Carol Sue with her again. It was much too dangerous. She would give it a couple of days and then return telling the Grandmother that she was going into town for supplies. She would then return and quietly check out the head of Turtle Wash. If she found Dante's body, she would know he was not the killer. She had to know, one way or another. She loved him. The thought of him using the body of Turtle Wash for a dumping ground was mind boggling. She could not tell law enforcement about the bodies of Millie or the Indian man. She had her own survival to think about. She had survived on Earth for centuries living hermit lives and staying clear of the law, dictators, and rulers. Her number one concern in her present existence was keeping Carol Sue safe and finding a way for them to return home to Planet Weelo. She would also take Dante with her, if he was willing to go. As of the moment, she had not yet told him she was an alien being.

~   ~   ~

Returning home, Moon Dance pulled Rosa's old, battered, green pickup into the parking area at the end of the travel trailer. She was shocked and surprised to see Dante at the other end cleaning wild rabbits. Moon Dance was furious. She had spent two days worrying about him and looking for him. Carol Sue was hungry, and she had almost confronted a murderer. In the moment, she lost it. His thoughtlessness, not returning home when he was supposed to, pushed all of her buttons, as humans said. She got out of the truck and slammed the driver's door. He looked up from skinning a rabbit and waved a bloody hand at her. A small, butchered, wild pig lay at his feet.

"Where in the Hell have you been?" Moon Dance screamed at him due to being over stressed, hungry, and frightened. Carol Sue slipped into the travel trailer ignoring them.

"Where have I been?" He huffed laying down the rabbit he was cleaning. "I have been hunting." He stated with a flushed face caused by eyeing the man's flannel shirt she had on.

"Hunting . . . ? You have been gone over two days and you have only two rabbits and a small pig to show for it? What have you really been up to, Dante?" She asked mad.

"Where you have you been and what have you been up to is the question?" He retorted angrily continuing to eye the man's shirt she had on. "Why aren't you inside getting ready? You have Tarot clients who will be here shortly. You look like you have rolled in some rancher's dirty hay and ran off with his work shirt. Do you have a bed with a ranch hand in it somewhere that I am unaware of?"

"You think I have been with a man?" Moon Dance huffed back as she considered his words. She was not happy about being accused of a cheap roll in the hay with some ranch hand.

"Why else would you come home wearing a dirty, man's shirt? It is not mine." He stated loudly and secretly jealous.

"As I recall, you did not want to come to my bed. If I want to sleep with a man, I will sleep with a man. You are the one who should be answering questions. You have been missing for two or so days. Do you have any explanation to offer? Carol Sue has gone hungry while I have searched for you, thinking you possibly had an accident or was dead in the desert. It should be me asking you if you have been in some woman's bed the last two or so days."She shot back in defense of herself."That would explain your not coming to my bed!"

Dante didn't answer. It was as though some deep dark secret was keeping him from responding. He picked up the two cleaned rabbits and pig, paused a moment, and then shoved them in her arms angrily and retorted. "I was hunting."

Then Dante walked down to the bank of the Rio, waded in, and proceeded to wash the blood from the rabbits and pig off of himself.

Moon Dance was furious! He hadn't the right to yell and accuse her of being with someone else. However, she did regret accusing him of being with a woman. He had been very faithful as a provider and protector. If he wasn't attracted to her, he had the right to turn her bed down. It was the fact that he had accused her of being with someone other than him that annoyed her.

For the next couple of days, Dante stayed clear of Moon Dance and he also stopped playing with Carol Sue. At night, he spread his sleeping rug in the pickup bed of Rosa's truck. Dante and Moon Dance entered a cold time of not speaking to each other, except what was considered civil in the presence of her Tarot clients.

On the third morning, very early and before Carol Sue and Song Bird were awake, Moon Dance couldn't take it anymore. It was time to make up with him. She bit her lip as she prepared to leave the travel trailer and go apologize for yelling at him. As she opened the door, she was shocked to see him standing there about to knock.

"Would you like to come in for breakfast?" She asked to break the ice. "I will fry one of those nice big rabbits you cleaned yesterday."

"I have no appetite, Rosa Moon Dance. I have something I must tell you." He replied nervously. "May we speak outside, so the grandmother and Carol Sue do not hear?"

Moon Dance stepped outside the trailer and closed its door behind her. The sun was casting an orange morning glow in the distant horizon, but it had not risen yet.

"If it is about our argument, Dante, I am really sorry. I was stressed over your being gone so long and I lost it." She quickly spit out.

"I am sorry too." He replied fidgeting. "However, that is not what I wish to speak with you about."

"If it is about the strange things going on in the desert, I am aware that there are people from our area that are missing. Carol Sue and I will be careful." She replied trying to make it easy for him to tell her about what part he was playing in the deaths in the desert."

"It is not about the gathering in the desert that is concerning me. I want to talk about our relationship."

"We have both said regrettable things. I am sorry and apparently you are to, or you wouldn't be here." She replied. "I have missed sitting with you on the bank of the Rio in the evenings and looking at the night sky."

"It is about my not sleeping with you that I wish to discuss." He spit out nervously.

"Do you wish to change your mind?" She asked breaking out in a smile.

"You were right. I turned your bed down and had no right to be upset because I thought you were with a man. I am sorry. Also, I wish to tell you that I have decided to move on in a few days, as soon as I have hunted and filled your freezer. It is time for us to give each other a little space."

"What?" Moon Dance asked in shock. That had not been the response she was hoping for.

"A man cannot enter your trailer and sleep with you if I am sleeping on a pallet blocking the door. I am not your husband or your lover. I have no right to make demands on you or keep you from seeing someone. I have decided it is best if I move on. I am sure I can find work on the Mason Ranch. He prefers older hands."

"You are an ass hole, Dante!" Moon Dance spit out in a harsh tone, thinking how she had just swallowed her pride in an effort to make up with him. She didn't normally curse, but he had brought out the worst in her. Then she burst into tears at the thought of losing him. He was the object of her new heart.

"I am not an ass hole, Rosa Moon Dance. I am a man who is choosing to stay out of your bed. I have my reasons. I will be leaving after I hunt for a couple of days. I will make sure you have plenty of meat in your freezer. When it is gone, you can replace me with the ranch hand and let him hunt for you."

Moon Dance was speechless. After their short conversation, Dante turned and left. They entered into a non speaking phase. He hunted nights and she lay awake waiting for the sounds of his returning. Moon Dance felt all the pain that goes with rejection. It was a second dose for her. Gray Feather had cast her aside to sleep with Pansy Skywalker and then Hissing Cat. Now it was Dante rejecting her and making her feel like she was not a desirable woman.

CHAPTER SEVENTEEN

The Unexpected Betrayal

It was late evening. Carol Sue had been put to bed and was sound asleep. Grandmother Song Bird was busy inside the travel trailer weaving a basket from grasses that grew on the bank of the Rio. Dante had filled the freezer with fresh meat as he had promised and was now packing his few possessions in preparation to move on. Moon Dance stood next to Rosa's green pickup and watched as he gathered up his things. He did not turn to look at her. Instead, he picked up his tattered backpack of belongings and walked out to the edge of the road, preparing to step onto it and walk away. He stopped with his back to her and stood for a moment or so. He didn't turn around and look at her. Moon Dance knew that he was going to leave her without saying good bye. It didn't get any worse than that. She burst into tears.

Dante took a couple of steps out and down the road. He paused again. Then he then stood for what seemed like an eternity with his back to her. Then, he turned around, stared at her, and set his back pack down. He then angrily kicked at a small stone that was on the shoulder of the road. Biting his lip, he then returned to where Moon Dance was standing with eyes full of tears. His eyes watered seeing that she was crying over him.

"I cannot leave you, Rosa Moon Dance. I love you too much." He stated with tears suddenly trickling down his face.

Moon Dance flung herself into his chest and he closed his seventy year old arms around her.

"I love you, Dante. I am sorry you think I want anyone but you. You are my god-send, my heart."

"I am sorry too, Rosa Moon Dance, with everything that is in me. I am sorry that I did not sleep with you when you asked. I wanted to. My heart does not know that my human body is old. My heart says I love you, like a man loves a woman. My old man brain and body tells me that I am way too old for you and that I should let you find a younger man. I have struggled with my attraction to you, ever since the day you pulled me from the Rio. I have been ashamed of my love for you. You are way too young in body and I am way too old in mine. Earth men will call me a pervert for loving you. I have questioned myself as to whether I am perverted."

Moon Dance whispered back to him as he nuzzled his cheek to hers. "You are my heart, Dante, my god-send. I do not see you as an old man. I see you as a man who has provided for me and protected me. I have fallen in love with that man."

"You are everything to me, Rosa Moon Dance. I feel guilty about not remaining true to my dead wife and children. Here and now, I want you, not them."

After Dante was pulled from the Rio by Moon Dance, he had told her that he had watched her from the Mexico side for a long time. He told her that His wife and children had all died in a flu epidemic and he had been left alone with no family. On the other side of the river he had decided to make his way to her and hope she would take him in and care for him in his old days. Rio Rosa had waved across the river at him for several years. He didn't swim the river till after Moon Dance had taken Rio Rosa's body as a host one.

"Your wife and children are dead, Dante. They would not want you to die old and all alone. Live the rest of your years in my arms. If your wife and children are looking down, they will understand."

"They are looking down, Rosa Moon Dance! Understanding my love for you is doubtful. However, I cannot fight my feelings for you anymore." Dante said. Then he stooped and picked her up like she was a child and lifted her over into the bed of the old green pickup truck which had been his bed during their cold war. His sleeping rug was still there. Dante laid her down gently on his woven matt. Then he climbed over the tail gate and lay down on top of her. In uncontrollable passion, he started running his weather beaten hand up her leg, pushing up her skirt. Then he made passionate love to her as the nights winds blew. Moon Dance let him ravish her. She was ready to be made to feel like a woman again. Gray Feather had been the last man she had slept with. Her new heart loved another. It was now Dante that she wanted.

In the back of Rosa's old green pickup truck, Moon Dance and Dante spent a magical night in each other's naked arms as the night winds blew.

Dante did more than make his Rosa Moon Dance feel like a woman. When she woke the next morning on the sleeping rug in the back of the old green pickup, the body of Rio Rosa was pregnant; although Moon Dance would not discover that fact for awhile.

~ ~ ~

Good things and good times don't always last. About three weeks after Dante and Moon Dance's first night of passion, the spring rains came and with it fierce lightning storms. On one particularly extreme and stormy night, Dante moved their trailer to higher ground knowing that the Rio was about to flood. Once on higher ground, Dante and Moon Dance stood in the open doorway of the travel trailer and watched fierce flashes of lightning streaking the sky and pounding the earth. Constant thunder sounded like cannons going off. The pair was not sure whether they had moved far enough inland. The sky was dropping water by the buckets.

As Moon Dance eyed the distant sky, she suddenly spotted a familiar sight. One of the flashes of fierce lightning was frozen in the distant sky and appeared to be suspended in the back desert, in the direction of Turtle Wash.

Look!" She shouted at Dante in sudden recognition. "It is the frozen moon-beam flash of lightning that Song Bird and I saw."

Dante stiffened up and put his hand over his eyes and stared at where she was pointing. Then, in a very nervous voice, he muttered, "They have come for me, Moon Dance. My tour of duty here is over. I am going home."

"What are you talking about?"Moon Dance asked turning and looking at him.

"I don't have time to explain, Rosa Moon Dance. I must tell you quickly who I am before I go into the desert and not return. They have come for me."

"Who has come for you?" she asked suddenly alarmed. He had a strange ex-cited look in his eyes. "Don't you go and do that disappearing into the desert act on me again, Dante. I love you."

"Do you believe there is life on other planets besides Earth, Rosa Moon Dance?" He asked nervously turning to her and taking her hand and holding it tightly.

"Actually, I do! Why do you ask?" She replied with her stomach knotting up. She wondered if he had somehow discovered that she was not human.

"If I told you that I am not a human, but am a being from another planet that lives in this human body, what would you think?" He asked holding her hand securely.

"It would be okay with me." Moon dance replied sure that he had discovered who she was. "Would you accept me, if I were a spirit being from another planet living in a human body?" She asked reversing his question. She feared his answer.

"I have a secret I have been keeping from you, Rosa Moon Dance. It is a secret you are probably not going to want to hear." He replied.

Moon Dance bit her lip. "Spit it out, Dante. I don't want any more cold-wars or arguments with you."

"I have lied to you, Rosa Moon Dance." He stated pausing for a moment and biting his lip. "I don't know how to tell you or have the time to explain. My wife is not dead. She is alive and I have five children." He stated quickly.

"What . . .?" Moon Dance managed to ask in a sudden moment of shock.

"The frozen moonbeam lightning bolt has come for me. It is a light port and I am an alien being from Planet Plutonia. I will be going home to night in the port." He spit out quickly while taking his finger and running it from the top of his head to below his belt buckle. The human body of Dante fell away and hung from his purple waist.

"Please pinch me and tell me I am dreaming." Moon Dance replied in an excited voice. She needed a Plutonian to grant her passage in a light port. From Plutonia, she could catch a flight on to Planet Weelo and decide for herself whether it had become a society of cannibals. Dante was the answer.

"You are not dreaming. I must be in the back desert and ready to board in an hour." He replied.

"We have an hour to get there?" She asked, suddenly in a great mood. She would grab Carol Sue and take her in her pajamas. Song Bird could have the trailer, pickup, and Tarot business.

Dante ignored the 'we' comment.

"Plutonian scientists and harvesters have been gathering in the desert for weeks in preparation to take this light port home. I am one of them. That is why I go into the desert to hunt and don't return when you think I should. We have been dismantling other light ports and getting all of our specimens and research crated so we can board quickly and not be taken by surprise by a possible sabotage invasion of cannibals from Planet Weelo."

The excited smile faded from Moon Dance's face. "You fear an invasion from Weelo cannibals; here on Earth?"

"Yes, so my planet is evacuating all of us scientists tonight. I thought I had a few more weeks to be with you and to break it to you who I am. The lightning bolt port has arrived early. I must board with the other scientists within the hour."

"Carol Sue and I will go with you. I am an alien to, Dante. See . . . !" She stated quickly unzipping Rosa's body so that he could see that she was a blue skinned Weelo.

"You don't understand, Rosa Moon Dance. My wife and children are Plutonian, not humans. I am going home to my wife and five children. They will be waiting for me when I exit the light port. They do not know about you. My Plutonian wife is not dead as I have always told you. She is very much alive and will be waiting to welcome me home."

"What about me and Carol Sue? What are we to you, excess baggage that you can just leave behind and forget about?" She asked with her excitement turning to anger. "You didn't tell me about a living Plutonian wife and kids before making love to me."

"You are Weelo and one of my planet's enemies." He replied reaching out and touching her blue filmy cheek. My planet fears an invasion by your race. They fear being captured and eaten for food. They fear your harvesters. You cannot go home with me, Moon Dance."

"You promised to love and protect Carol Sue and me forever." She replied in shock with the whole situation becoming clear to her. She had been used. Gray Feather had betrayed her old heart and now Dante was doing the same to her new one. Both had lovers that she knew nothing about or was too blind to see.

"All Plutonian light ports on Earth are closing tonight. They may not be opened again for hundreds of Earth years. War is on the verge of breaking out in the heavens of our home planets. This is my last chance to go home. My harvested specimens are crated and probably loaded by now into the frozen moonbeam lightning bolt, light port. I must go home. I am sorry I have not had more time to spend in your bed loving you."

"Explain to your plutonian people that I have not lived on Weelo for almost three thousand Earth years and I am not a threat or part of Weelo cannibal society. I may have blue skin, but I am not a cannibal."

"It is not just your skin color, Rosa Moon Dance. I have a wife and five children on Planet Plutonia waiting for me to return. They do not know about my affair with you. I have fallen in love with you and Carol Sue and you two have helped me thru many lonely hours here. However, I love my Plutonian wife and children more. I want to go home to them and resume my life. You have to let me go home to them." He stated with tears in his eyes. "I am asking you to love me enough to let me go home alone, Rosa Moon Dance."

Moon Dance removed her hand from his.

"Your light port may be my last chance of ever finding a way to get back home to Planet Weelo. I want to go home as much as you do. I can't believe you are denying Carol Sue and me that privilege." She retorted in shock.

"My family would never understand my exiting the light port with you, a blue Weelo on my arm and in my bed. Besides, there are guards on the port doors. They would not let you on due to your skin color. As hard as it is to leave you behind, I must."

"You are disrespecting and abandoning me just like my New Mexico tribe once did." She muttered in disbelief and disgust at herself for ever loving and trusting him. All the painful emotions concerning Gray Feather's betrayal swept over her.

"We have been good together Rosa Moon Dance. However, I must go home now to my wife and children or I may never see them again. I have to choose between you and my wife and between loving one child here or five there."

"How can you abandon Carol Sue and I, knowing you will never see us again?" She demanded in a very hurt voice.

"I love you Rosa Moon Dance, but home with my wife and five sons is where I want to be. I want to resume my respectable life there and watch my sons mature, get married, and give me grandchildren. I am just forty years old there and in my prime. I have a lot to offer my family and my planet. If I stay here, I will have to keep reincarnating in human bodies that are sometimes less than desirable. Dante the peasant man has been a hard existence. On Planet Plutonia, I am respectable, fairly wealthy, and do not have to sleep on a pallet or eat wild rabbits and snakes. My scientific mission here on Earth has been a great adventure. However, it is not what I want as a permanent life for myself. I want to go home to who I really am; a respected scientist, husband, and father on Planet Plutonia."

"So, all I have been to you is just a mistress, the one who is expendable when it gets down to the nitty-gritty of things?" She replied cut to the core of her being.

"It is a hard choice, Rosa Moon Dance. I must wake Carol Sue and tell her Goodbye. I have just a little less than an hour to make it to the light port and board."

"You are an unbelievable Jackass, Dante. What makes you think I will let you wake up Carol Sue and break her heart like you have done mine? I will not let you tell her that you have five children alive somewhere that mean more to you than her. She loves you and has accepted you as her father. I will tell her tomorrow that you died in the desert while hunting tonight. She can learn to live with that. That lie on my part is more respect than you deserve. I will let her spend a lifetime having good memories of you. I will not have that option. I will remember you as a man who used me and lied to me telling me his wife and children were dead. Get out of my sight, Dante. You are lucky that I don't kill you and let Carol Sue's dog be the cannibal that eats you."

"I am sorry I gave in to my passions and made love to you. I was trying to walk away from you before we crawled into each other's arms. I thought we possibly had a few months or a few years before the last port home would appear. Had I known that I would be boarding my light port home so soon, I would not have slept with you. I was trying to be faithful to my wife on Plutonia when I was walking away to go work on the Mason Ranch. I am sorry I slept with you."

"You have disrespected me in the worst way by not telling me you had a living wife and children. I won't forget. Should I ever find a way to journey to Plutonia, you are guaranteed that I will tell your wife of our affair and the baby of yours that my human body now carries."

"You are pregnant?" He asked looking at her with disbelief in his eyes.

"I will also tell your wife that you disrespected me and didn't tell me you had a living wife and children when you crawled into my bed. Then I will dump this baby in her lap and leave it, so it will become a lifetime wedge between the two of you. I am sorry I rescued you from the Rio."

"Get an abortion, Rosa Moon Dance. A mixed breed child here will have no life. It is over between us, Rosa Moon Dance. That is how it has to be."

"It is not over, Dante. One day I will find a way to Plutonia. When I do, I will disrespect you as you have done to me. It will be your chosen wife and sons who will feel the pain that Carol Sue and I will now suffer because of your disrespect." She spouted in anger, while realizing that he was just another version of her nightmare, Gray Feather. How could she have been so stupid as to think that he wanted and loved only her? He didn't love her. She was just a mistress to him, a body to use.

Dante then turned from her, walked away into the rainy night, and disappeared. This time he did not pause and look back. He kept on walking.

~   ~   ~

Once, out of sight in the desert, Dante discarded his human body and then in a flash, flew off into the desert to take the last Plutonian light-port home. He did not look back. Home on Plutonia was where he wanted to be. Perhaps, it was a selfish decision on his part, then on the other hand, possibly a good one. Only time would tell.

~   ~   ~

Moon Dance stood in the doorway of Rosa's travel trailer with blowing rain drenching her. She cried and replayed in her mind his words of choosing someone besides her. Gray Feather had chosen two besides her, Pansy Skywalker and Hissing Cat. Jack Benson had cursed her by returning her heart. She now cursed herself for the fool she was. Then, the human body she was in gagged. She threw up from being pregnant. In the moment, she didn't know whether she wanted to live or die. How was she going to explain an unwanted pregnancy to those who came for Tarot readings and explain who the father was? There was no explaining that she was an alien and now carried an alien child by a scientist from Plutonia who had deserted her.

Standing on the step to the travel trailer in the drenching, pouring rain, she turned to go back inside.

Suddenly, she was startled by the angry voice of a woman behind her.

"You took my body without my permission. Give it back." A familiar voice demanded.

Moon Dance spun around in shock and was face to face with the pink human spirit of Rio Rosa, Night Hawk's witch.

"I . . . I couldn't find you when I returned here to take you up on your terms and offer. I healed your stab wounds and have kept your human body alive and functioning. I have been baby-sitting your body for you." Moon Dance spit out, not knowing what to say.

"Did you make Night Hawk think I was in love with his brother?" Rio Rosa demanded in a slightly calmer voice.

"Night Hawk is missing, Rosa. He walked out into the desert after Millie's baby was born and never returned. He is assumed dead." She replied. "There was no need for me to pursue a relationship with White Eagle."

"Why is my trailer inland and on higher ground?" Rosa asked floating around it and peeping in its windows. Then she asked loudly and with disgust. "What is Song Bird doing in my trailer? She hated my guts and plotted to break me and Night Hawk up before Millie stole him from me. I am going to kill her for daring to sleep in my bed."

"White Eagle became the owner of the ranch when Night Hawk disappeared. Song bird heard and saw hummers. White Eagle had her committed to a mental institution. She climbed out a window and then made her way here to me, thinking I was you. She has nowhere else to go." Moon Dance shot back, not knowing what she was going to do about this unexpected turn of events.

Then Rosa was really mad. "What is that child doing in my bed next to Song

Bird? This is a Tarot reader's travel trailer home, not a nursery or an old folk's home."

"Well, Rosa, get used to your home being a nursery. I have some news that you are not going to want to hear." Moon Dance muttered rolling her eyes and thinking that she might as well just get it over and tell Rosa that her human body was pregnant.

So, Moon Dance quickly told her that she was pregnant by a lover that had jilted her. She did not tell Rosa who.

"Oh my Catholic God . . . ! I will be lucky if the priest lets me in the confessional, much less listen to me confess." Rio Rosa shouted in disbelief. "Don't you know what birth control is?"

Moon Dance closed her eyes, bit her lip, and didn't answer. Rio Rosa had a right to chew on her.

"Who is the girl?" Rosa once again demanded.

"She is the daughter of a peasant man named Dante. He went hunting in the desert and died there. She is a border crosser and has no one. I have been watching out for her." Moon Dance stated telling Rio Rosa as little as possible and lying where it was necessary. "Her mother died giving her life. Her father swam the Rio and I rescued both of them as they were about to drown. She has been with me for months and has no one to return to Mexico to."

"Are you telling me that, not only am I pregnant, but I have two extra mouths to feed? One is a child and the other is an old woman who is a runaway from the crazy house?"

"You will soon have three extra mouths to feed; Song Bird, Carol Sue, and the baby your body is pregnant with. The baby is due in about eight months." Moon Dance replied knowing that she was going to have to return her human host body to Rio Rosa, as well as give her the love child that she and Dante had made. The giving up of the baby was bittersweet.

"Well, crawl out of that body and let me resume my life. I hope you haven't run off all my Tarot customers." She replied in a disgusted voice. "I will have to do a lot of winning at the poker table to feed the lot you are leaving me with."

"I think you will be pleased with the increase I have made in your clientele." Moon Dance shot back. Then she took one finger and run it from the top of her head to the crotch of her human host body and then unzipped it as though it were a dress. She then stepped out of it in her filmy blue form and let Rio Rosa's human body fall to the desert floor. "Treat the little girl well till I return for her. Tell her that Dante, her father, will not be returning and has died from a hunting accident

140

in the desert."

"Well, at least you are returning for one of them." Rio Rosa replied rolling her eyes in disgust.

Moon Dance ignored her remark and said, "Before I leave, Rosa. I have one last thing to do."

"Do it quickly before I take a chill from this rainy night or get hit by lightning. This is a god awful storm and I never remember seeing one like it in all of the years that I have lived on the banks of the Rio Grande. Is God mad at you over something other than your promiscuity and love affair?"

Moon Dance ignored her ranting questions and reached down and removed the Indian boy's necklace from her discarded host body. She then entered the travel trailer for the last time. She walked back to the bedroom, in her blue Weelo body to where Carol Sue and Song Bird lay sleeping. She noticed that Song Bird's long braid, with the feather tied in the end of it, was coiled with the tail and feather hanging downward off the bed. The coil looked remarkably like a dream catcher, except there was no web. She draped the necklace thru and around the coil of braid and secured its clasp. If it was Song Bird's missing daughter's necklace, she would recognize it. If not, she would probably think it was a gift from Carol Sue or possibly Dante, whom she would never see again.

Then Moon Dance returned outside and shot off into the night sky, heading for the back desert. She had to find a way to board that light port, if she had any hope of going home to Weelo. She would return for Carol Sue when she found a way to do so. She cringed as she considered the fact that there was the possibility that Carol Sue would grow up thinking that Rosa was her mother. However, there was one good thing to come out of her existence as Rio Rosa Moon Dance. Carol Sue would have a little brother or sister to play with. Hopefully they would bond and be close.

CHAPTER EIGHTEEN

The Zookeeper's Grin

On Planet Weelo, Gray feather stood naked at the front of his cage, leaning on the rocked wall that separated his and Ralph's cages. He listened, trying to decide where the zookeeper was. He and Ralph were not allowed to speak to each other. There were no sounds being made anywhere and he surmised that the female keeper was possibly on break or feeding animals elsewhere, if there were any.

"Ralph, are you there?" Michael Gray Feather Haven shouted in a low voice.

"I am here." Ralph stated reaching his hand out thru the bars of his cage and around the rock wall to where his friend Michael was. Michael took his hand and held it like they were tiny boys playing, or brothers watching a scary movie back on Earth. They were past the stage of pretending to be macho, hand shaking men.

"I am afraid that our turns are going to come up today." Dr. Michael Haven, or Gray Feather, whispered. "If they come for one of the children, we must beg them to take us instead. We are the last two of those arriving here on Noah II. As far as I know, all have been sent to the rumored slaughter house. "

"I know Michael. This is probably the last time we will ever speak to each other. You do know how much I love you as a friend, don't you?" Ralph Archer asked squeezing his friend's hand.

"I know, Ralph. You have always been there for me. Thank you for being my best friend and brother. I know we are not related, but I have always thought of you as my brother. We have been thru so much together." Michael whispered back not letting go of his friend's hand. He needed the comfort of it. He was facing his mortality.

"We have definitely been thru a lot of crap since that fateful day in Bullhorn, Texas when I dumped my blonde bimbo fiancé at the altar and we ran wearing goose feather wings. I am really sorry I got you mixed up in that. Had I not fell for her charms in the bedroom, you and I would probably still be back in New Jersey and running our vet clinic. Even better, the two of us might be on holiday somewhere skiing."

"That is true, but which two of our friends can say they have been on holiday to Planet Weelo?" Michael added with a sarcastic laugh. Then he added. "Which of our colleagues can say they have stayed in an all nude hotel with rooms that are cages and maids that are aliens?"

Ralph snorted and again squeezed his friend's hand.

"What two doctors can say they once wore angel wings made out of goose feathers?" Ralph retorted snorting. "

"You got me on that one, pal." Michael laughed. You did strut your stuff wearing those wings just before we made a break for it! You seemed to always have a knack for having more fun than me. I was the vegetarian stick in the mud that always put a bit of a damper on everything. Had I kept my mouth shut and let you marry the blonde bimbo, we might not be here right now."

"Actually, Michael, I wouldn't trade a minute of this crazy alien adventure with you. We have lived comic book lives here. The only thing missing is a masked, capped, hero or heroine who rescues us."

"You have always been my hero, Ralph. I have just never said anything. If you can't rescue us from this crazy comic book adventure, no one can."

"If today is the end for us, I want you to know that I don't regret all that we have been thru together. You are the best friend a man could ever have. We made a lousy decision as scientists and doctors to board that space flyer and then Noah II. However, that is what life is all about, making decisions and following dreams. Our choices have landed us here. At least we are experiencing our comic book nightmare together. I wouldn't want it to be any other way. If we have to die today, together is how it should be." Ralph stated.

"I feel the same Ralph. If I have to be eaten by cannibals, I would rather it be with my best friend accompanying me. Ask the cannibals, if you get a chance, to leave the salt off when eating me. I don't want to feel responsible in death for raising their blood pressure."

Ralph snorted. "If you get the chance, tell them to leave the pepper off of me. I would hate to die thinking I burnt the hell out of their hemorrhoids as I passed thru."

"Do you believe in God, Ralph?" Michael asked getting serious. "I recall when both of us were Catholics and afraid to marry knowing we only got one shot in the marriage department. I have really screwed up up in that department. I had a child by one, married another, and was in love with a third. I think I might be on the crap list of our Catholic God."

"Well friend, I think you and I are the gods in our lives. We are the creators of our current shared Hell. Do I believe in God? I don't know anymore, Michael. I do know that I believe and trust in you. I have not seen God. You I have seen and you have always been there when I needed you."

"I have done some serious praying the last few months asking God to spare the lives of the children. My prayer for Carol Sue was not answered. She died in the slaughter house months ago. Today the others may do the same. Where is my Catholic God or the Great White Spirit that the Indians spoke of on the reservation in New Mexico? Both seem to have a deaf ear turned to me and my prayers." Michael asked in a voice that choked up.

"I have asked myself the same questions, Michael. I imagine all of the Jews that died in Hitler's gas chambers and camps asked the same questions. I don't know why God seems to have his back turned on us, or if he even exists."

"I have made a bargain with God, Ralph."

"What is that, Michael?"

"If somehow you and I escape this hell we have walked into, I am going to return to the church, take vows, and become a priest. I have even vowed to never speak of Moon Dance again, if he does so."

"Wow . . . I didn't see this one coming! You . . . celibate?"

"Bargaining with God is all I have left to try to protect all of you and get us out of here. Either God comes thru for us, or we are steaks for the cannibals dinner tonight. There is no one left to help us now, other than Him."

"We have done a lot of things together, Michael. I think I will pass on the priest thing." Do you really think that today is our final day?" Ralph asked in a serious tone.

"There were only three visitors to the zoo yesterday. I have done everything, including doing handsprings, to keep the public interested and amused with me. You have done the same. I think hunger and the search for meat is now dulling the need for amusement in the public's eye. Yes . . . I think today is the day."

"Do you regret marrying Hissing Cat in the desert, Michael? Moon Dance and her arms were just over the dune waiting for you."

"I have regretted a lot of things, Ralph. I was a stupid young jackass that made a lot of bad choices. On Earth we can divorce our bad choices and start over. Pansy Skywalker tricked me into sleeping with her. Carol Sue was an accident. Hissing Cat tricked me into marrying her by having her girl tell me that Moon Dance was dead. I was a fool twice. I wish I could divorce those two bad choices and walk away from them. The love of my life, Moon Dance, killed herself over my bad choices. I have had a hard time dealing with that. I really was in love with her. It was her that I wanted to be with, not Pansy Skywalker or Hissing Cat." Michael replied. "What about you. Do you regret anything?"

"I regret marrying your girlfriend Jennifer after you came up missing. We were consoling each other's loss, ended up in bed, and then married each other in a mutual drunken moment. Neither of us expected you to come back knocking on our door three or so years later. I have always felt guilt about that and the three children I have by her that probably should have been yours."

"If it makes you feel any better, Ralph, I would never have married Jennifer, even if I hadn't disappeared. She was pretty on my arm, but I was not in love with her. Moon Dance is the only woman that I have ever been in love with. I honestly don't know what I was thinking when I hooked up with Pansy and then Hissing Cat. Moon Dance was my heart. If there is an afterlife, maybe I will join her there before the day is over. Hopefully, she will forgive me."

"With your luck, Michael, we will probably get rescued and you will have to become a priest." Ralph shot back.

"I am tired of this cage, Ralph. I am ready to let go. Death has to be better than standing here naked like an animal with women staring at my body parts all day."

"Don't give up, Michael. No visitors to the zoo means that wars for food is about to break out in the streets. When chaos reigns in the streets, the zoo keepers will run for cover to save their own flesh from being eaten. There is a possibility that we might escape these cages and hide till the cannibals have consumed each other and they are down to the last man. We can eat our own fecal matter to survive if we have to."

"Your plan for our future dinners sounds really appetizing Ralph." Michael replied almost gagging at the thought.

"I know how we can survive a little longer Michael. Are you game?"

"Lay it on me. I have run out of ideas."

"In my opinion, we should offer the zoo keeper sex or anything that will buy us one more day or week of life. Weelo women are not allowed to sleep unless they are awarded that right as a sort of bonus for being productive in society. Meaningless cage cleaners, like our female zookeeper, are rarely afforded that bonus. I think we could pimp ourselves and maybe save our lives and possibly the children that are caged on further down from us. The three black haired babies and my three kids deserve more than to be eaten like Thanksgiving Turkeys. We might be able to be save them from the slaughter house, if we play our cards right this morning."

"What do you have in mind? I hardly look like a calendar playboy this morning. I look more like an ape that hasn't had a bath or a shave in months. My toenails and fingernails are claws, not to mention that I haven't seen a tooth brush since arriving here."

"I have watched the tall one, who is on duty today, eyeing us. I bet she is an old maid who has never been in bed with a man. Sex with her may be our key to staying alive a little bit longer. Weelo is populated almost entirely by women. We, as males, are a rarity. That is why the women have made their way here to stare at us, up till now. We are the forbidden fruit. Only the elite and professionals are permitted to mate. In my opinion the elite are trying to produce a race of super intelligent women. Those of less intelligence are not being allowed to reproduce."

"Being a gigolo is a definite step down the ladder for us, Ralph." Michael retorted in disgust. "Can't you come up with some other plan to save us, the babies, and your kids?"

"Take it or leave it, pal. I think we have just found our last niche in society on Planet Weelo."

"I still don't see why the zookeeper would want to sleep with us? We have been in these cages for months with no baths or clothes. We are hardly sexy looking in our dirty birthday suits."

"It is not our birthday suits that the zookeeper keeps eyeing, Michael. I think we should make gestures at her of a certain nature. It just might work and buy us a little more time. I, personally, am willing to do anything if it will buy my children even one more day. I think our six foot six zoo keeper, down deep, is wondering what it would be like to be mated with us. She may have only seen one or two males in her lifetime and those two are us."

"A man has to be attracted to a woman to make love to her." Michael retorted. "She definitely is not my type. Also, she is at least a head and a half taller than me. I would be sticking my nose in her belly button."

Ralph laughed before continuing. "Our current survival does not depend on the zoo keeper being our type. If she goes for your gestures, just close your eyes, do your thing, and pretend that it is Moon Dance in bed with you."

"I get your point, pal! Who are you going to pretend she is, if it is you she chooses? There is that possibility."

"Moon Dance . . . "Ralph replied laughing.

"What . . . ?" Michael asked in shock.

"Since this is possibly our last day together and you are thinking of becoming a priest, I have a confession to make. Hear me Father Michael."

"Drop the crap, Ralph, why Moon Dance?"

"Back in New Jersey, you returned telling about a mystical medicine woman you had met and fallen in love with by the name of Moon Dance. I was fascinated with your stories about her and also jealous. I was unhappily married to your girlfriend, Jennifer, whom I did not see as a gorgeous woman of mystery. I think I fell in love with your Moon Dance thru your tales. We have always done things together. Why wouldn't both of us fall in love with the same woman? It is who we are and have always been."

"I didn't expect this confession, Ralph. Are you serious?"

"You are the last priest I will probably ever have the chance to make a confession to. Yes, I am serious. Forgive me father, for I have sinned. I have been secretly in love with a woman other than my wife and she is my best friend's love."

"If God hears me and I have to keep my vow and enter the priesthood, you would run off with my Moon Dance, if she were alive?" Michael questioned in disbelief as he made the sign of the cross.

"Like you say, we each make our choices. Now, it is time for us to try to find a way to survive another day. Sex with the zoo keeper may be it. If she chooses you, just pretend she is Moon Dance. Make passionate love to her and her belly button. Make it so good that she won't want to see you sent to the slaughter house. I will do the same if she chooses me."

"The question is which one of us will she choose?" Michael Gray Feather Haven retorted thinking about his vow of future celibacy.

"We have always been competitive. Let's seduce her like it is a game to see which one of us wins." Ralph stated and then laughed. "Whichever one of us wins, loses. She is no prize."

"What about North Star? The two of you were an item in the desert before leaving Earth." Michael asked.

"She was my Hissing Cat. What more can I say. You and I both were fools." Ralph replied. "She was my momentary madness."

"She is coming. Get away from this wall Ralph." Michael stated and then he quickly moved to the center bars of his cage. Human specimens were not allowed to have contact with each other, unless there was a reason. The zoo keepers decided if there was reason. Ralph did as he was told and moved to the center bars of his cage.

When the six foot six, female zookeeper walked in front of Michael's cage, he took a deep breath and then flashed her and grinned. Ralph did the same when she passed his cage. To their dismay, she walked past them and seemingly paid neither of them any attention.

When she disappeared out of site, they both returned to the rocked dividing wall and continued their conversation while laughing.

"I think I have lost my sex appeal." Ralph stated with a snort."Have you got any suggestions?"

"She walked on by me too." Michael laughed. "Have you got any suggestions?

"Only that we try it again the next time she walks by."Ralph retorted.

"Apparently she likes to look at us, but she isn't attracted to us," Michael replied.

About that time, Michael heard the door in the back of his cage being unlocked.

"Oh God, Ralph, she has chosen me."

"And me . . . "Ralph replied hearing the back door of his cage being unlocked. "Don't blow this Michael, no matter what she asks you to do. She is our ticket and the children's to surviving a little longer. We have just become caped and masked gods. It is up to us to save the children and any other human in this zoo that we are unaware of. Pretend the zoo keeper is Moon Dance and this is your wedding night."

"Pretend she is Moon Dance . . . pretend she is Moon Dance." Michael muttered as he watched the six foot six, blue skinned zookeeper enter his cage with a smile on her face.

Do Gray Feather and Ralph Long Legs barter their male charms in exchange for survival rites for Ralph's children, the black haired babies, and the other caged humans in the Weelo Zoo? Does Moon Dance stow away in Dante's light port, in an effort to return to Planet Weelo? Does she tell Dante's wife about their affair? Do Gray Feather and Moon Dance find their way back to each other, or does Dr. Michael Gray Feather Haven become a priest?

READ THE NEXT BOOK

"DANTE'S SORROW"

Alien Encounters, Book 4

www.ingramcontent.com/pod-product-compliance
Lightning Source LLC
Chambersburg PA
CBHW051249170626
46809CB00004B/1566